PRAISE FOR ENSLAVED

I felt like I was reading my own thoughts while reading about Ava's meetings in the Pentagon! If you only knew how true it is?! I'm already hooked on this series and I can't wait to learn what unfolds in Ava's love life, spiritual journey, and professional aspirations. Let's make this into a movie already! I met Ericka, the multi-talented author and mother of two adorable dogs, when we started our fellowship at RAND Corporation in Santa Monica, CA. Our group of research fellows were all pretty exhausted from our demanding careers. Ericka and I began our real-life spiritual awakening during that year. I have a sneaky suspicion this book series is only the beginning of what's to come from her. **—Lieutenant Colonel Sherry K. Oehler, US Army, Professor of Military Science at the University of Arkansas at Pine Bluff**

Ava's life opens the door to a much-needed conversation on self-love. Her struggles with love for self, life, work and her lover hit home for many women. So often we burry the hurt, and embarrassment of not measuring up to the outward illusion we've crafted for the world to see. Journeying into Ava's world provides a safe place for women to connect with these feelings. The preview of book two promises hope for Ava and I am eager to discover how her journey unfolds! **—Treneice R. Flowers, Esquire**

This book is...relatable, hilarious, heartbreaking, captivating...I found myself telling other people about it and what I had most recently learned about Ava...and most of the folks I talked to wanted to read it based on what I told them. I think it is very relatable...and just as sad as it is funny. It is a really nice mix. **—Trish Eagan, Book Reviewer**

This book is EVERYTHING! I loved it and read the entire book in one sitting. I opened this book and could not put it down. It is funny. It is relatable. There is a little of Ava in all of us. We are aware of what our desires, dreams and aspirations are but too comfortable with the known, mundane parts of our lives to make a change. She is scared yet bold. She is sassy yet growing into her confidence. The book provides humor in an all too real story of not living out your dreams. I can't wait to share this book with my friends. I am sure they will love it just as much as I did. This book is truly amazing!! **—T.A. Book Reviewer**

ENSLAVED

The Lady and Her Pentagon

A Novel

Ericka Reynolds

CSL Infinity

The views expressed in this novel represent the personal views of the author and are not necessarily the views of the U.S. Government, the Department of Defense or the Department of the Air Force. This novel is fiction and all characters are fictitious. While there is mention of federal buildings, agencies and companies all characters are derived from the author's imagination to prevent Personally Identifiable Information violation. Any resemblance to persons either living or dead is coincidental.

A special thank you to Loni Love who inspired the character Monique. Your story of following your heart's desire has inspired me greatly!

Dedication

Don't let the black woman in chains fool you.

This book is dedicated to those who want desperately to follow their dreams, but are still holding themselves back.

Yes, I am a black woman—an African-American woman, to be exact or politically correct—but this mindset goes beyond the image on the cover. I hope this story will touch everyone who has imprisoned herself or himself in something that they know is not right, be it their job, their romantic relationship, their relationship with God, with their friends, their children—or with themselves.

Acknowledgements

Special thanks to those who contributed to the book cover:

Brittany N. Adams MS, ATR, LPC – lady in chains photo
Maryann Walker (Facebook) – bio picture
RhoyalD_MUA (Instagram) – makeup, bio picture

ENSLAVED

Prologue

I am about to take the Hemings tour at Monticello. On the bus ride up to the house I overhear this conversation between a mother and her daughter, who is around ten years old:

Mother: You know Thomas Jefferson didn't free all of his slaves when he died.
Daughter: I'm sure there was a good reason.
Mother: Maybe they didn't want to be free.
Daughter: That seems unlikely.
(Me, thinking): This is going to be a long day...

But, as I exited the bus it hit me: maybe they *didn't* want to be free. Not because freedom wasn't desired, but because freedom was an unknown.

Heck, I slow down in my writing practice sometimes, which I've accepted as fear of the unknown. Not to sound vain, but I know my writing will take me out of my familiar life of being a government employee and catapult me into a great but yet so unknown world that it scares the crap out of me.

I believe there are other reasons that Jefferson didn't free his slaves when he died, including, very likely, that they were part of his children's inheritance, and it was known he was in debt, and those slaves were sold to settle part of that debt. And, most certainly, he didn't take a poll to see if they would have liked to be freed.

But I digress. This is about fear. It's about seeing what lies ahead and not stepping forward into your vision. Imagine that you are atop a mountain looking out at forty miles of beautiful landscape. This is what the slaves at Monticello would have seen. But, should you have envisioned a life beyond that mountaintop, should you have dared to reach out to have a life beyond your current existence, you would have been hunted down and beaten to near death.

You are trapped. You are enslaved.

How, though, does this differ from today? You are young; you are black; you are stopped by a police officer. You have a clear vision of what lies ahead; your home, your family, your future—but you are trapped. Should you move, physically or verbally, you too will be beaten to near death or killed. You are enslaved. You are one hundred-plus years past the existence of slavery in this country, and yet you must watch every move; must not appear to step out of line; must not appear to envision a better life.

Have we progressed? Have we?

I am free, am I not? Yet I live like an enslaved person or a black youth of today. I might not have fear of the overseer or the cop following me down the street, yet I don't move forward towards my vision.

I exist on my own plantation, my own self-imposed prison. I call it Shawshank. The rest of the world calls it the Pentagon.

PART I

{A WEEK IN THE LIFE}

1

Between the Sheets

~

My body is glistening with beads of sweat as he pounds me from behind. I glance back to look at him, to catch a glimpse of his hot, sexy, naked body. Our eyes meet and he forces a passionate kiss on my lips. Moaning with passion he slowly pulls out of me and commands me to take in his full length into my mouth. I do so with great pleasure and as I do, his moans become louder and louder. We are so freaky with our sex and I love it. He has now pulled out of my mouth and lowered his body underneath me. I ride him with delight as I move like a jockey coming across the finish line. Our eyes meet again and I lean into him. I kiss him long and hard and he returns my kiss with radiating heat, first my lips, then my neck, his tongue melting into my hot sweaty body as I gasp to catch my breath. We both reach our climax and as we do I open my eyes, turn off my vibrator, and place it on the nightstand.

That was a good one, Shemar Moore, but time to end this fantasy. Baby Girl has got to get some sleep. My prison time at the Pentagon starts in a few hours.

Doing Time

~

Merriam-Webster defines "slavery" as:

1: drudgery, toil (or, my daily existence in the Pentagon)

2: submission to a dominating influence (as in, my selecting a major in college that would make my parents happy so they would pay for my room and board as I only had an academic scholarship

And "bondage" as:

1: the tenure or service of a villain, serf, or slave (or, my entire existence in a life that I hate)

And "imprisonment" as:

1: to put in or as if in prison: confine (as in, my self-infliction of mental pain and anguish by continuing to live a life and work at a job that I hate)

I could keep going with "captive," "confined," etc., but the bottom line is that I'm living a miserable existence. Grateful, though, for my job and the life it affords me, but otherwise, miserable, as I know I was meant to do something drastically different with my life.

Many people refer to the Pentagon as a prison (though I'm the only one that I know of who actually calls it "Shawshank"). I think that comes from what it looks like on the inside courtyard, reminding you of an exercise yard in a prison, and I think people feel like it's a punishment to come here because, well, at least for the military folks, it marks the end of the youthful part of their careers. Sure, we have a few captains and three and four stripers, but for most, it's the end. Especially for our pilots. They come knowing the odds of flying again are slim, which means they're old. It means they will go off and be squadron commanders, then wing commanders or other things; they might even become generals, but the love that they had for flying has now been laid to rest.

I've been serving time in the Pentagon for eight years. While some would say it's honorable to serve at the highest level of our nation's Defense Department, I don't view it that way entirely; I am honored to serve, but I hate the conditions. My work life is a combination of the movies, *The Shawshank Redemption* and *Groundhog Day.* Polar opposite genres, but, well, that's pretty much how it is—a never-ending sentence and repetitious crazy.

I moved to the DC area from Oklahoma City in July 2007 with big dreams. I remember driving down the interstate blasting the best of the '70s on my iPod and sipping on my coffee. I was as carefree as I could have ever imagined. My dad had warned me a few nights earlier that when I crossed the Oklahoma state line I was finally going to break down and cry. It would be at this point that I would come to my senses about quitting my job and moving across the country to start a new life. I did recall our conversation, but only as I crossed the Virginia state line, and I had no regrets.

I'd already spent twelve years in a job that I hated, but stayed because everyone said I was really good at it. And I'd waited nine years for the man I loved to realize that we were right for each other because everyone told me we were right for each other. But he never did, so after twelve years of a thankless job and nine years of a thankless man, I packed up and headed for greener pastures.

As I pulled up to my new apartment in DC, there had still not been one teardrop during the two-day journey. It was safe to say I'd made the right choice. Life is too short to spend it waiting around for things to get better where you are, so if you want a change, make it. Get up and do something about it. I'd spent my entire adult life doing what everyone else told me was the right thing to do. I majored in accounting because my parents told me I needed a good job when I graduated Alabama State University, moved to Oklahoma because my career counselor told me I wouldn't be offered a better job coming out of college, and pursued romance because everyone said the next step after landing this good ol' government job was to get married and start a family. So with all those things not working out, I decided to start anew.

Here I was, Ava McClure, a thirty-four-year-old independent woman making things happen! Working in the Pentagon! Just call me the modern day Mary Tyler Moore; living in a fantastic city, meeting new people, having a real life! Who would have thought this would be happening to me? Not Ava, not the one everyone tried to convince she was making a huge mistake by leaving Oklahoma. A friend even called my parents and asked them to tell me to stay. I am not sure if he really thought this would work, but he called and pleaded his case to my folks. My dad said he was touched by Gerald's concern for me. My mom just thought he was nuts. Gerald's wife scolded him for trying to disrupt what the Universe had for me, and all the while I was operating on autopilot looking for a place to live during my house-hunting trip to the District.

Fast-forward eight years and here I am. No better job, no man except my real-life fuck buddy, Dan, and living in Virginia, not the swanky District. And, most importantly, not pursuing my dream of being a successful writer, something I was sure would happen once I move to the big city.

Mondays

~

Mondays are the best and the worst here at Shawshank. It's like someone hits a reset button and all the work you did the week before is OBE (Overcome By Events). But not to worry, someone will come up with an idea two weeks later and it will look and feel a lot like what you were working on before, but this time you'll be tasked to do more, like set up an IPT (Integrated Process Team), a retreat basically, from the other crazy assignments you have to work on. People will fall into place in some conference room once a week and rattle off all they know about the subject at hand, but no one will ever really do any work. But, it's a nice way to take a working break, drink your coffee, and commune with your fellow co-workers/inmates.

Unfortunately I don't have an IPT today. Today I have the pleasure of being a slide flipper for my 2-star (or "Major General," as I say when addressing him). We are working on our 3-star's (Lieutenant General's) pet project. I get the pleasure of setting up the room beforehand, as this is what middle-grade GS (General Schedule) employees do here. At the base in Oklahoma I was a big dog with a secretary; here I'm just Ava, the do-everything and know-everything and the "we wouldn't be doing shit without you but we are going to treat you like a nobody (though you are a somebody because we give you awards all the time even though they are meaningless)" employee.

I enjoy having light-hearted conversations with folks as I distribute the binders and handouts around the conference room table, as it takes my mind off how much I really don't want to be here. Plus, the room is nondescript, so there's nothing to evoke any upbeat feelings. Every conference room is decorated the same: brownish-colored walls and Air Force Blue curtains with a picture or two hanging on the wall, maybe a legacy wall with pictures of past DCSs (Deputy Chiefs of Staff).

Seeing Frank, a middle-aged white guy who looks beat down every time I see him, makes me smile. He actually gives a damn about what goes on here, as I once did. I seem to have lost any zest for this place, and I'm twenty years his junior. Back in my earlier days I was badass Ava. "The Bitch," they would call me. The "get-your-shit-together-as-I-have-mine." Sadly I believe most still see me this way, but I know it's just a facade. Sure, I still have senior leaders who call me their bulldog, but the thrill has long been gone.

"Good morning, Frank. How was your weekend? I see you're here early."

"Another wonderful Air Force day."

"Ok, so does that mean you had a bad weekend or too good to tell?"

"What? Oh, sorry. I'm just used to the generic response we give around here. My weekend was great. I took the wife to a B&B for our anniversary."

"Wow! That sounds nice!"

The room is beginning to fill up with generals, colonels, and other civilians, and I have had it with this old computer system, but whatever...maybe we'll have slides projected or maybe we won't. I can hear my 2-star arriving, Major General Mark Deeds (or "Maj Gen Deeds," as we would refer to him in our mountains of memos and reports, or simply as "my 2-star" when I'm talking about him at happy hour. That last term is the way we casually refer to our bosses among ourselves, but never to their faces in the hall), so I just need to keep focused.

Here he comes. Short, overweight, and stuffed in a flight suit. There really should be some rule that if you are not slim and/or buff you are forbidden to wear these things. They certainly were not designed for the five-foot-four-inch, I-would-appear-to-be-pregnant-if-I-weren't-a-man, don't-fly-no-more pilot.

"Hello, sir. I have your materials on the table."

"Thanks, Ava. You are so efficient. I never have to worry when I know I'm going to a meeting that you're in charge of."

"Thanks, sir."

It takes all I have most days to muster those words. Looking at Maj Gen Deeds with that aloof grin makes me what to scream. He truly is a character. He looks like what Dennis the Menace would have grown up to be had he eaten at McDonald's every day and stuffed himself in a flight suit. If you look closely you can find one or two strands of blonde hair, but mostly he's all white up top. He's a nice enough man, but my distaste for this place makes him seem like a jerk to me on most days.

A lieutenant colonel (Lt Col) enters the doorway and announces the 3-star general: "Ladies and Gentlemen, Lieutenant General (Lt Gen) Green."

Everyone rises as the general enters. You can always tell the truly modest ones from the ones who just pretend to be. The modest ones walk in, get to their chair, and then politely tell everyone to please have a seat. The vain announce this command as soon as they walk through the door. I think they get some thrill out of giving us the command to sit, and they like to draw attention to themselves, hence the "everyone please sit" announcement before we can even see them enter the room. I wonder if others have figured this out. Lt Gen Green is the latter.

I will say, though, he is very attractive, if not all that bright, so at least I have his looks to get me through meetings. He's a six-foot Latino hottie who clearly works out regularly. He's actually biracial, as his father is white. I know this because he made a point last year of giving us way too much of his life story during Hispanic Heritage Month. Anyway, I just know he's easy on the eyes.

"Everyone, please take your seats. So, Ace Boom"—which is Maj Gen Deeds's call sign—"how are we coming with this project?"

"Going great, sir! Just here today to give you a quick status update. We first want to take you back to the original concept of this project..."

I am sitting behind Lt Gen Green, and am all ready to flip sides, and now this bullshit. Why? Why in the hell do we need to do that? This man has been here since day one and it was his idea to move in a different direction; heck, it's all his idea! This is supposed to be a status meeting. I freaking hate my job! This could have been covered in the weekly staff meeting, but Ace Boom here needs his face time, his brown-nosing, ass-kissing face time. And, oh, by the way, I hate call signs. I've never bothered to research or ask about the history of them; I just know they are ridiculous.

"So, sir, if you will recall...Ava? Can you give Lieutenant General Green the background on this project?"

I wish I could kick his ass.

"Certainly, sir. Sir, this project was the direct result of your innovative" (bullshit) "notion to track the number of taskers" (which are the pain in the ass requests for information or coordination on something that is hardly ever used for anything important, whether a response to a Congressional question or a review of some new or revised policy or regulation that no one reads, and when they do, misinterpret for their own use) "we actually meet on time as a way to boost morale" (never mind that every suspense—which is the due date for a tasker, which most view as a negotiation point for when something is actually due—has no impact on national security or the aid of our allies and partners or anything else of real relevance) "and this project was to help highlight when we do something in a timely manner and/or satisfy a member of Congress with an answer they accept."

"Why, yes, then I thought we should change it to how often we are late on taskers because that motivates folks much more."

"Of course, sir. The briefing we have for you today shows we are down in our numbers and your expected results are not quite there yet."

"Thank you, Ava. So, Ace Boom, since this is our number one priority…"

(You have got to be fucking kidding me.)

"…I think it's time we have an All Call" (an extremely long and uncomfortable meeting that is supposed be informative on some level, and, I'm guessing through osmosis, boost morale) "about it, plus, we are two quarters behind on handing out awards, so assemble the masses and put something together that shows how serious this is."

"Will do, sir."

"Around the room? Anything to add?"

Why do they do this "around the room" thing? They don't give a shit about what we think, yet, here it goes. Lt Gen Green smiles as he makes eye contact with everyone at the table, each of whom replies "no," and then he gives those seated in the Peanut Gallery a once-over, as if he cares about their opinion.

"Well, thanks, everyone."

Lt Gen Green rises to leave and the room stands at attention, and… wait for it…

"Carry on."

We are now free to be free.

Wonder why he doesn't tell us to carry on as soon as he says "thanks," like when he enters, he tells us to sit. Just a thought.

"Well, that went differently than I imagined," says Maj Gen Deeds.

"How so, sir?"

"I was hoping he would see this idea sucks and stop."

"I would have just told him that if I were you, sir. Sometimes they need our help. I would have offered that up, but I don't think it's my place."

"Not your place! You're the one who told our Vice Chief he was holding up the process on approving those new regulations. Don't tell me you're afraid to give it to a 3-star."

"Well, sir, that's a good point. Perhaps I'll let Lieutenant General Green know in the near future."

As I am collecting the papers left on the table I can tell Ace Boom is contemplating something.

"Good idea! Try to do that before this All Call. We really don't need to go through that."

"Sure, sir, I'll do my best."

"Great. I'm out for another meeting."

Why is it that I'm the lowest ranking person here, and yet I'm expected to do the hard shit? Anyway, I am sure I can bring it up in another meeting, and see if I can get Lt Gen Green to drop this nonsense.

As I turn off the projector and walk to the door, it hits me that it's only Monday morning, 0810 hours. I turn off the lights and close the door and run into my friend, Terry, in the hallway. I like Terry. She's down-to-earth, but knows how to hang with the best of them in this building. She reminds me of Marla Gibb's character, Florence, on the television show, *The Jeffersons*—full of sass but somehow manages to keep her job. I think she might weigh 120 pounds and that would be great if she weren't five-feet-ten. She looks like skin and bones. I think, though, the curly, fiery red weave she wears, which complements her high yellow complexion, somehow balances her out. I wish I had her height. I'm just five feet tall and I am hitting the max weight for my height at 125 pounds. I fill out my suits nicely, but any more poundage and it's a rap. I alternate between weaves and wearing my hair relaxed in a shoulder-length bob. I'm not high yellow, but I'm not mocha either—my makeup color is Golden Tan, at least, according to Bare Minerals.

"Hey! How's it going?" I say to her.

"Hey! Another great Air Force Day!"

"Really?"

"Really. What else am I supposed to say?"

"I don't know…how about, 'how's it going'."

"It's going. I have a Joint Staff IPT where no one is going to be prepared to discuss anything and it's scheduled for two hours, so I am going to have a late lunch because I have another meeting right after this and I woke up late so I missed breakfast and it's that time of the month and I'm feeling really bitchy. Is that what you wanted to hear?"

"Ah, yes! Truth!"

"And how's your day going?"

"Another great Air Force day! Ha! Seriously, I just left the dumbest meeting of all time."

"Not possible. The day's still young."

"No, we prepped for days to brief our 3-star on his pet project that sucks, and we were only in the room for ten minutes."

"So, what's his pet project?"

"Oh, you are going to love this! He's tracking how often we are late on taskers so he can use that to motivate his people. Wait, before you say anything, yes, we started out tracking how often we were on time, but he thinks pointing out our incompetency is a much more effective method, and sadly, he really believes this shit."

"Well, are you really surprised?"

"No, I am just tired. Eight damn years of the same old fake-ass, Stepford-smiling, bureaucratic robots who come in here day after freakin' day not doing shit that matters and collecting a paycheck. And then there's you and me and a handful of people actually give a shit and work on projects with the belief they could matter—but in the end, what? Nothing, that's what. You know how the Honor Guard always states on those tours that there are twenty-some thousand people who work here?"

"Yeah?"

"Well, I truly believe only about five of them actually know what's going on. The rest of us are just here keeping up appearances."

"Probably. You need a happy hour. You know it's been a while. Yep, I'll send an email out today. We could all use some decompression time. Where do you want to go?"

"I don't care."

"How about that new restaurant in City Center? Oh, I can't think of the name, but yeah, that's it; a happy hour in the city's newest revitalized area! Awesome, right?"

"You mean re-gentrified, right?"

"I mean I need to get to this meeting, so slap on your Stepford grin and have a wonderful Air Force day!"

I watch Terry walk off, and turn down a corridor. She's so skinny her skirt has twisted halfway way around her waist. I'd tell her, but she wouldn't care. I walk a few paces and then turn around and go to the restroom. Once inside I drop my papers off on a shelf and then enter a stall where I stand for a moment with my head against the door. I begin to say my daily prayer: "Lord, I know this is not what I was brought to this earth to do. Please help me."

I open the bathroom stall, wash my hands, and head out of the restroom. As I walk down the corridor I pass a group of black guys talking. They are decked out in their Steve Harvey suits. I'm sure they've noticed Mr. Harvey has changed his style, but maybe they just like this look or they paid so much for these suits they plan to get their money's worth. What impresses me the most is how black we are here in the Pentagon. People would probably be amazed. We don't turn down our blackness at all. Well, in meetings we do, but in the office and the halls, *we are turn't up.* At least there's some freedom in that.

4

My Office

~

As I enter my office, I see my colonel (Col), David ("Sledge") Baker, an extremely tall Asian man who is also biracial—something I found out during Asian American and Pacific Islander Heritage Month. I think next year during Black History Month (and yes, I still call it "Black" not "African American"—I'm just old school that way), I'm going to tell folks about my half-white background. I'm not biracial as it relates to my parents, but I think it might just be a fun fact to let them know that I'm about 100 percent convinced I'm the product of non-consensual sex from slavery, as I am on the fairer side of brown. I wonder how that would go?

"Hey, Ava! How'd it go?"

"Lieutenant General Green wants to have an All Call to better convey his vision for this project."

"Oh, I see. Well, I'm glad you're handling it."

"Sure. How was your meeting, sir?"

"Oh, I didn't have a meeting. I just didn't want to go. I trust you, so no need in tagging along. And, let's be honest, this project is crazy!"

"Oh, okay."

Ain't that some shit. How about if *I* just don't go next time?

I head to my cubicle and see Al. Al is a lot of fun to sit next to; he's really levelheaded, a quality seemingly missing from many around this place. Plus, he's always hipping me to the Latino culture.

"Hey, Al. What's up?"

"I'm working on some charts for Lieutenant General Green's meeting with OSD (the Office of the Secretary of Defense)."

"Is this about the state of our aircraft fleets?"

"Yeah, that's it."

"I can't wait to see the finished product."

"Sure thing. What about you? Are you done with that crazy special project?"

"Not even close, but I have got to get back to my other stuff. I've got that partnership meeting with Policy (an organization within OSD) later this week, and I'm missing coordination from most of our MAJCOMs (Major Commands of the Air Force)."

"Really? Why?"

"Because none of them are buying off on our way-ahead-for-our-partnership strategy. They think we are overlooking some countries and giving too much attention to others. Plus we're not the boss of them. You know they only report to the Combatant Commanders most of the time."

"But aren't they just supposed to buy off on what type of support they can provide?"

"Yes, but everyone wants to have a say. Goldwater-Nicholas means nothing to anyone."

"Yeah, that's true. Combatant Commanders are supposed to be in charge, but the Army, Navy, and we are still burying our heads in the sand like the change never happened."

"Yep, we got a lecture last week from J5 reminding us we are only here to OT&E (Organize, Train and Equip)."

I give Al a smile and turn to start working when my phone rings. I notice the number and take a deep breath. It's Marcy from Policy, one of my least favorite people. Why? Because she's a bitch, plan and simple. She's one of the ones who believe they are actually in charge of something, but has no clue what in the hell is going on. She's young and lacks any knowledge of the DoD, but she's here as a political appointee, so we must tolerate her.

"Strategy, this is Ava. Hi, Marcy! How are you?... No, I don't have the package ready from our Chief; I told you that Friday evening... Well, yes, it *is* now 8:45 on Monday and nothing has changed...I understand...The SecDef is wheels up in four hours, but I can only do so much...I'll keep you posted."

I hang up the phone and look blankly at Al.

"I love the 'wheels up' threat!" he says with a sardonic smile.

"Funny how that means absolutely nothing to me anymore. I get that the Secretary needs a coordinated position before he lands in Africa, but the Chief won't sign off on the position until our Intel guys are happy with the wording, and they are not happy, and couldn't care less about when the Secretary is wheels up. And you know what? Neither do I. The Chief's exec is leaning hard on those guys, so why should I play middle man?"

"Cause Marcy's not going to let up until you get her what she wants."

"Well, today is the day Marcy gets to see what happens when I don't care."

I give Al a huge grin as I spin my chair back to face my computer and begin working.

THE DAY PROGRESSED without much further drama, which is nice for a Monday. I've decided I've done all I can do and start shutting down my computer. I hear Col Baker on the phone, so I try to stall. He's usually the first one out of here, so it's unusual that he's still around. I don't really want to risk being bothered with him on the way out, but my babies need me to get home to them...here it goes.

"Good night, sir."

"Good night, Ava."

"Sir, so you know, our Intel guys signed off on the position prior to the SecDef's departure."

"That's good. Would have been a shitload of more work had they not. Thanks for staying on top of that."

"Sure thing, sir. Goodnight."

"Hey, do you have a copy of the brief that went to the SecDef?"

"I don't have a hard copy, but I can email you the slide deck."

"Great, can you do that before you leave? Major General Deeds just called and wants me to come up in a few to discuss."

I know he sees this bag on my shoulder.

"Sure thing, sir."

Why can't I ever just leave the office? I shouldn't have mentioned the Intel guys…and the freakin' computer is so slow it's probably still stuck in shutting down mode. I walk back to my desk and drop my bag on the floor. I turn on the monitor and see that the computer is indeed still in restart mode. I sit and wait. And wait. Finally, I can log on.

"Hey, Ava?"

Why is he back here?

"Yes?"

"Hey, while you're up and running again, can you type up a few notes for me to discuss with Major General Deeds?"

"Sure."

"Great. I'm on in ten, so it doesn't have to be much."

"Yep, okay, sir."

"Thanks!"

I once went to the doctor about my chronic headaches. He took out his prescription pad and wrote me a prescription that he said would cure any future headaches. When he handed me the sheet it simply said "no."

I should have kept that and taped it to my desk. Oh well, I am most upset that my dogs are waiting for me, poor things. I'll be home soon, babies.

Okay, Ava, he needs this in ten. Just type some quick shit up and jet out of here. *Key…Takeaways…from Review…of Project X…*and…done.

"Sir, I sent you the brief and some talking points."

"Awesome, thanks! Have a great night, Ava."

"You, too, sir."

I head out of office and down the corridor. I scan out of the building, say goodnight to a Pentagon police officer, and head out the main doors to exit to the Metro. The plus side of staying late is the train is less crowded; the negative side, my bus from the train to my house stops running as frequently. I think I should get the dog walker back on a recurring midday schedule. It's expensive, but my babies shouldn't have to be punished for my lateness.

The bus is late and I am tired and ready to get home. I overhear the most bizarre conversations at the bus stop, plus, regardless of when I exit the train and walk over here, there always seems to be the same old man who tries to flirt with me. Maybe it's just my imagination. The bus arrives and I can finally sit for a few minutes. It's quiet and, today's my lucky day, the old flirt is nowhere in sight. Exiting the bus and walking to my house feels like miles, but it's only two houses from the stop to my house. I should really consider moving into the District, but I love my little 1950's bungalow rental in Alexandria, Virginia.

I'm just so tired, mentally, that is. The streetlights are on and this alone makes it feel as though my evening is already lost. The summer has come to an end, as we just celebrated Labor Day last weekend, and while I love the fall, the slow onset to another Daylight Savings Time saddens me. I think I suffer from Seasonal Affective Disorder, though I've done nothing over the years to validate this or find a way to help myself.

"Hello, ladies! My sweet babies, my little angel babies! How are you?"

Seeing my baby dogs always brings me back to life. I have a ten-year-old black toy poodle named Cleo and a nine-year-old Yorkie named Sophie. I've had them since they were six weeks old and they have been my constant companions ever since. Men have come and gone, but these little loves are my life.

I need to check my phone to see if my fuck buddy is coming over. I sure hope not 'cause I am not in the mood for him. I need to get rid of him. I think I am still holding out the hope that this will turn into something more, even though Steve Harvey made it very clear in his book, *Act Like a Lady, Think Like a Man*, this would not be the case. But, Dan started off saying he wanted a relationship, saw me as the mother of his children, talked about us as an old married couple, and then one day, I suggested we have wild and crazy sex in his new condo and he freaked out and said he couldn't breathe around me and only couples did things like that but the day before he had just asked me if I was okay with the fact that his new place only had a shower and not a tub. Seems like I just don't get it with him, but I have some hell-bent desire to make it work. I'm pretty sure it's because I have commitment issues of my own, something I discuss regularly in therapy until I decide I'm good, and stop going for a while. But this is not an issue today because there is no missed call from Dan.

"Well, no daddy Dan tonight! Who's ready for dinner?"

My dogs eat better than I do. Holistic everything and free-range chicken is common for them. As for me, all my ingredients come from whatever was on sale at Wal-Mart. Dan once noted I have several sets of ceramic dishes for the dogs, yet I cook my dinner using pots and pans from the dollar store. He thought I should treat myself, so I purchased new cooking utensils from Williams-Sonoma. The prices were so high I thought about not getting them, but then, when I thought about how much I paid for the dogs' dishes, beds, clothes and toys, I thought, well, I can afford to treat myself once in a while. It's funny how I put myself after my dogs. I am pretty sure that's not normal, though probably is something that is done by many, so I'm not alone.

My dinner tonight is a meatless meal. I tend to stick to a meatless Monday thing in hopes of working my way to vegan someday. I've been at this for a while and so far I haven't moved past Monday with the meatless concept.

My home is cozy and fits us well. I was fortunate to find it as a rental for such a low price—three bedrooms, two baths, a beautiful sunroom, and a large backyard. I've kept my big, chunky furniture from Oklahoma, all of which is walnut in color and looks like it belongs to a couple in their sixties and not a forty-one-year-old single woman living in Alexandria, Virginia, but nonetheless, it's mine and it's me. And, it's on this taupe-ish-colored, hobnail-studded couch that I will eat my meal and watch *The Young and the Restless*. It's my guilty pleasure. Every night while I eat my dinner and play with the dogs, I tune in for another episode of mediocre drama. Dan used to come over almost every night and we'd cook together. Damn, I was really duped on that one. Anyway.

After dinner, playing with the girls is a great stress release for me. I think they know how much this helps me because—okay, I don't have a clue how they know, so I'll just say it's a great stress release.

"Okay! Who's ready for some fun?"

I CALL MY time out of the building my "reverse work-release program." By day, I am a prisoner of Shawshank and by night, I am free to pursue my true love of writing. I think we're all imprisoned in some way by that place. In eight years, I've never heard anyone say they are happy to be there, neither the military nor the civilians; they all talk about seeing better days on the other side of the building or during their military career. For the military, I can see the desire to be done. So many deployments, so much time away from family, but when they are done, many just come right back as civilians or contractors, the double-dippers. I used to really wonder about this group, but now I get it. We are all imprisoned, be it the car we can't really afford, or the alimony we are now paying, or the children that need tuition paid. We are all there because we can't leave. Service to our country is great, and don't get me wrong, there is pride in what we do, but if any of us won the lottery or the Publisher's Clearing House, I'm guessing the majority of us would quit.

Anyway, I digress. I love to write and have been doing it since I was seven. I wrote and illustrated a book in the second grade. My teacher loved it (or so she said), laminated it, and bound it with yarn and read it to the class, and afterwards placed it in the reading corner. I was so proud. I don't know if most kids take their free time on a weeknight to write a book and then bring it to school the next day, but I did. I once wrote a screenplay and sent it to Diana Ross when I was twelve, but she never wrote me back.

Somehow I am digressing again. My current work is children's literature, though I never finished my last project, which was a novel that got great reviews—from my girlfriends. They are my cheer squad, telling me how my work will free me from my current daily existence. I know they believe this, but sadly I don't really believe it myself. I want it, but something keeps me from claiming it. Every year a few of us go to the National Book Festival and every year I make my pledge that one day soon I will be one of the featured authors. Every year they tell me how they will be there with front row seats cheering me on and every year we go and I'm still no further along toward realizing my dream. Funny how they believe in me more than I believe in myself, even knowing that I tend to start and not finish the things that are most important to me. As much as I have become jaded by the Pentagon, I see it as a safety net; while I truly dream of writing, in reality, I only play around with it, and always wake up the next day to do the job I have no desire to do.

Tonight is no different, even though I just received some awesome feedback from an actual literary agent who thought my children's books (once completed) would be a hit. As I sit here in my home office typing, I know I will be impressed by what I write tonight, but then will find an excuse to stop and pull out some work I brought home and focus on that instead.

Here it goes…"Okay! Who's ready to hear this version of *The Adventures of Cleo and Sophie*! I've made some edits and I'm feeling really good about this one!"

I love reading to Cleo and Sophie as they curl up by my feet under the desk. They are a great comfort, and I know they want the best for me. And, maybe they know this book is about them, so they've got a vested interest. But even they can't prevent the inevitable…

"Okay, now who wants to review the new Air Force Instruction Manual that's due for coord by next week?"

Eventually, it's time to shut things down; it's getting late. I turn to the girls and say in an excited voice: "Let's get ready for bed! Night-night time!"

I say this every night, and every night these two jump up and race to the back door for their last potty break with more excitement than I can muster up about anything. I think they're excited to sleep with me, though I am sure they sleep most of the day anyway, but they know this is their cuddle time with mommy.

As we return from the backyard, I turn off the lights and set the alarm. It's now time for my nightly ritual of a scalding hot bath and candles. It's a must every single night I'm here alone, which is one of main reasons I'm good with no Dan tonight. Sitting in this very hot water discoloring my skin is by far the best thing in the world for me. I soak and I reflect and I find my peace.

5
Tuesday

~

I'm a snooze-aholic. I will hit snooze until I begin to feel guilty, knowing I could be late for work. And, I can't possibly ever get up before hitting it at least three times. I once owned a radio alarm that had a remote. That was a nice deal. Hit the snooze button on the remote that was on the pillow next to me. Way too easy—it was for the best when it stopped working out of the blue.

Before I open my eyes, I say the same thing every morning: "Lord, thank you for another day of living, for your grace, mercy, love, blessings, and support." Now the day can begin. I've been doing this for years now. It's my silent morning praise and I don't believe I've ever forgotten to say it.

"Good morning, baby girls! Are you ready to go potty?"

As my girls hop down from the bed and follow me to the back door, I realize that today is a Dr. Smith day. She's my therapist. She's an elderly white lady who's crazy as hell, but I love her. She curses and fusses and gives it to you straight. As much as I love to support black businesses, I would feel awkward spilling out my life to an African-American woman or man. I believe it would feel too shameful, too embarrassing to spill all my shit to another black person. I should probably talk to Dr. Smith about this, and ask her what is up with that? Why would I feel inadequate around my own people? Anyway, I think I had some homework from the last session, but I didn't really do it. Once I leave Dr. Smith's office, I hop on the Metro or get in my car, depending on my mode of transportation for the evening, and think about the assignment during the ride home, and then I usually forget about it after that. It's sad because I'm really pumped up for those thirty minutes on the train or driving home in silence, and then it's like, I'm good, I'm okay, I'm fixed, and then I question if I even need these sessions, and then I see Dan and I realize I'm not any better off, so I return for more therapy.

"Here's your breakfast, ladies! I think today I'll skip the oatmeal and get something with grease in it at work. What do you guys think? Probably not a good choice, but it will make me feel good for a moment."

I've managed to pull together an outfit, a black sheath dress and a canary yellow short sleeve sweater. I tend to stretch out summer for a long as I can, as most women in the building do. I won't be back to basic business suits until late October. And no panty hose until the temperature is in the 40's—something I picked up from Michelle Obama. She once noted not liking hosiery and only wearing it when the weather called for it. Made sense to me, so for me, forty degrees and below is my stockings threshold.

"Okay, bye-bye! See you later! Home on time! Love you!"

As I'm locking the door, it occurs to me that since I am supposed to see Dan tonight, I need to call the dog walker and have her give the girls an evening walk and their dinner. And, I just lied to the girls and said I'd be home on time. I feel very guilty for that, but I'm glad I'm still able to use the dog walker for short notice visits

I am not a fan of the bus, but it's the price I pay for living in the country, as Dan calls it. He's from Chicago and says he could never do the suburbia thing. I told him the country doesn't have a bus stop two doors down the street or a Metro stop a mile away; nevertheless, he's unmoved, though he frequently likes to tell me about homes for sale in this neighborhood. I know he wants this kind of life, but he's so stuck on keeping up appearances as this big-ass city guy that he'd rather suffer in the District.

Speaking of the commitment-phobe, I see I have a text: *I've been thinking about you all night. I can't wait to get balls deep in you tonight.*

Why can't I love myself enough to do better than this shit? I really should do my homework from my therapy sessions. I text Dan back as I exit the bus and walk to the Metro platform: *I can't wait to have your dick deep down my throat.*

Gee, I really need to do better. As much as we learned about self-esteem all throughout middle school and high school, and I can self-diagnose my issue, I just can't seem to fix it.

I HAVE A love/hate for the Metro. I love that I get on at King Street and there's always a place to sit and I get to read the *Express* paper. Hate because at Crystal City, it becomes sardine city, which shouldn't bother me, since I'm only two stops away at this point, but people are so fucking rude, and I am just pissed off by the time I get off at the Pentagon.

As I exit the Metro this morning and enter the building, I see two Air Force guys huddled up by the jewelry store. (Yes, we have a jewelry store in the Pentagon, and it has a great deal on watch battery replacements: $7 per watch every Friday.) I think the men in the building gossip more than the women. It's pretty shameful how they go about it. Most like to do the "look over their shoulder and then proceed to the low voice that's not really a whisper," and of course, they are standing in the middle of office, being obvious. Perhaps women should school them on the proper way to gossip, like in the restroom or over lunch. I don't doubt that the guys gossip during these times as well, but middle of the aisle that flanks twenty or so cubicles is just wrong, and standing in front of the jewelry store is no better.

I try my best not to participate in gossip, and do a really good job of not spreading any, but this place seems to make that mission challenging. It's not that we gossip about people and their personal lives; that would actually be more of a normal thing. No, we chat it up about the wrongdoings of others—who got passed over for promotion, who is a complete idiot yet just pinned on their first star. I don't doubt this type of chatter happens in corporate America, but for us, it just seems extra sad because at the end of the day, we all are paid about the same and have the same level of responsibility and there isn't really the path to some great thing like in the outside world. I do the work that equates to that of a member of the Senior Executive Service (SES) General Officer Equivalent, for those who don't know. I say this because my SES is constantly delegating things to me that include briefing the Vice Chief of the Air Force. Now, they get paid about twenty grand more than I do, but the way I see it is, I can always bug out and they are the ones holding the bag, though it's not my nature to do that, so I'm pretty sure I'm just getting used and not compensated.

To illustrate, I once had this conversation with a co-worker:

Brad: "Hey, Ava, you have a dog walker, right?"

Me: "Yes."

Brad: "Why?"

Me: "Because I work late most days."

Brad: "And why is that?"

Me: "Because I have too much on my plate."

Brad: "Have you ever thought about the fact that if you let some of your work fall through the cracks that they would see how much work you actually have and would give you some help?"

Me: "No, that has never occurred to me, but that's a good point."

Brad: "And, you don't account for all these extra hours?"

Me: "No, I don't log any comp time."

Brad: "So, you pay someone to walk your dogs because you do the work of three people and you don't even get compensated for it? If you went home on time, you could save hundreds of dollars or you could at least collect comp time for your effort, but you don't; does that make sense to you?"

Me: "Now that you say it, no, it doesn't."

Brad: "Just something to think about."

Me: "Yeah, it is."

I'd like say that was a wake up call for me, and it was, for a minute, but my level of dedication to something I loath is quite impressive to me. I wonder why that is? Slaves worked hard or got beaten. No one is going to beat me. No one is even going to fire me. If they tried it would take years; I know, as I once tried to fire one of my employees. And while they were working to get me fired, I'd just file a grievance and more than likely win after years of litigation, and by the time it was all over I'd be able to retire anyway. Damn, I hate this place.

I did mention Brad's thoughts to Maj Gen Deeds, though, and he quickly changed the subject. Not surprising, of course.

I said, I wonder why that is, but I know. I do my best to please people who don't give a shit about me. It's part of my makeup. It's some complicatedness from my childhood. All I ever wanted was to be noticed by my parents. For them to take a second from doting on my sister to see me, but that never happened. I learned to fry chicken when I was ten. I cleaned and washed clothes, I took an interest in my dad's Army life as a little kid, even letting him run his Drill Sergeant commands on me for practice, but in the end, it was always her, my sister, who got whatever she wanted, never got a spanking and was the princesses of the house.

Now, don't get me wrong, I got things. I had more baby dolls than should be allowed. They heard me when I said what I wanted for my birthday or Christmas and they acted accordingly. But we all know gifts don't replace love. I am happy to say we are in a much better place these days, but I still see the favoritism, and the sad repercussions it has on my sister; in a way, I'm good. At least I'm independent, even if probably too much so. I have a wall up and a moat surrounding me that keeps me either alone or in emotionally unavailable relationships. (There's a book entitled, *Actually, It Is Your Parents' Fault* by Philip Van Munching—I always highly recommend it to everyone I know.)

But I digress. I do that a lot. I have way more thoughts in my head than should be allowed. I've tried meditation, but I can't seem to get that going for me—bought a book, set up a room, lit candles, and nothing—so here I am, in my world of thoughts, and my lonely life.

6

Therapy

~

"Ava?"

"Yes?"

"Ava, you just stopped mid-sentence. Would you like to finish your thought?"

"Not really. I just really hate my job, but for no good reason. I mean it's easy enough and I'm given all kinds of liberties to do whatever I want with any assignment I am given, but it's just all meaningless. You know what I mean?"

"I do, but that's not what you were talking about. You were talking about your relationship with Dan. You were hitting a breakthrough and then you just stopped."

"Ah, yes. Dan is an ass and every man I've ever dated has been an ass. I see now that I was attracted to men who were much like the members of my family. It's not that they were good for me, but that's what I was familiar with. I know I want love and I chase after it, but I set my sights on emotionally unavailable men, which is reflective of my relationship with my family."

"Ava, that's a great discovery! Now we can give you the tools you need to move past this."

"Is it, though?"

"What do you mean?"

"Now that I know why I do what I do, how are we going to work on me not doing it? And why?"

"What do you mean, why?"

"I don't know what I'm saying. It's been a long day. I'll see you next week."

"Wait. I don't have any more patients. Maybe we should continue."

"Naw, I am going to head to Dan's and have a long night of sex with him before I learn of these tools that will get him out of my life and leave me sexless for a while. Have a nice evening!"

"Ava, really?"

"Yes, really. I know we go through this every time and I learn ways to love myself and want more for myself, but then I fail. I really want to try *to try* this time, so I'm just going to have one last hurrah."

"How do you think that will make you feel?"

"I will probably not feel anything but the sense of another body which, honestly, will be enough for tonight. You know, I once dated a crackhead."

"No. You've never mentioned that."

"Yeah, I met him when I first moved to Oklahoma. I was slow to realize he had a drug problem, but when I did find out, I thought I was supposed to save him. Anyway, he has been the only guy that I found no comfort in sleeping next to. Not because he was a crackhead, though, but because he was an abusive ass. I couldn't stand him, but I couldn't believe that anyone else would ever be interested in me. It seemed like I was stuck."

"Ava, that's very interesting. Do you see any similarities between your feelings then and now?"

"Same lack of self-esteem many years later. You know, it took his dad coming over to see me and tell me to kick him out of my apartment for me to let him go? How sad is that?"

"Sometimes we just need support, and it seems his dad was that for you."

"Yes, he was, but why couldn't I have enough feeling of self-worth to get rid of him? And even after that I took him back a few times before I finally was able to let it go, and in the end it was he who left me. How sad is that? I got dumped by a crackhead."

"Does this change your mind about seeing Dan tonight?"

"No. See you next week."

And there went another breakthrough that will be a faded memory by next week's session. Oh well. I really do want to do better. Sometimes I think Dr. Smith should just prescribe an antidepressant or something. Maybe if I was legally high I could just walk the fuck away from Dan. Maybe.

As I head to the garage I check my phone, hoping Dan has canceled, but no. To say Dan and I have a complicated relationship would be a lie; what we have is a fucked-up relationship with a lot of bullshit that revolves in and out of it—it's really just me settling, me not having enough self-love.

I see a text from the dog walker letting me know the girls have been walked, fed and played with, and were chilling out in the living room when she left. That's good, but I still don't want them to be alone for much longer tonight, and I do deserve alone time, though that would probably be better spent at a spa than at Dan's.

Dan lives in a very nice part of the District, about two blocks from the White House. I'm sure he purchased a condo in this area to show off to his family and friends. He's quite the narcissist. I hate calling him on this damn phone directory. It always takes two or three tries and I feel foolish yelling in this intercom.

"Ava! Come on up!"

I do love his building. It's rather swanky, with an industrial look to it. It looks like something that should be in SoHo or Brooklyn, not two blocks from the White House.

I'm not sure why every time I get off the elevator Dan is taking out the trash. Is there something about ringing the bell he doesn't like? Strange…wonder why he can't just open the door and let me in, but we always greet in the hall as he's walking to the garbage shoot.

I exit on the eighth floor and see Dan heading to the trash shoot.

He greets me with a soft kiss on the lips. Damn, he's sexy. I hate this. I hate this because he's fine as hell. Six feet tall and beige, curly hair, and a body that's ripped. Not Mr. Universe bulky, but slender with muscles rippling in all the right places. And yes I said beige, not to be confused with high yellow. I still sometimes question my attraction to him, as I am a lover of the super dark brother and the blonde, blue-eyed fellow— yes, complete opposites—but there's no denying Dan's hotness. I think it's that Chi-town swag that turns me on. Today he's wearing khaki pants, a red and white plaid button-down, and loafers with no socks. He's always nicely dressed, which I don't get since we are just fuck buddies. Seems like it would be okay if he were wearing sweats, but he never is.

"Hello, sexy. How was your day?"

"It was okay. How was yours?"

He opens his door and gestures for me to enter. As I do, I turn to face him and see he is unzipping his pants.

"Well, I know how it can be better than just okay."

I give him a half smile and then lower myself to my knees to perform oral sex on him. As I take him deeper into my mouth, he grabs hold of the kitchen island and moans. I inhale and intake all of him and I am rather proud of my skills. I take a breath but before I can continue he takes hold of my hands, pulls me up and leads me to the couch. I unbutton his shirt and he slides his pants off. He slides my sweater off then turns me around to unzip my dress and while teasing me with soft kisses on my neck, pulls my dress and panties to the floor. He moves back up my body tracing my inner thighs with his tongue, now his tongue is on to my back and my body is beginning to heat and pulsate as he unhooks my bra.

My body is hot with anticipation; I am on my knees with my hands gripping the arm of the couch. I brace myself for his growth as I feel him enter me. Dan loves doggy-style and I'm all about it; while it's not very intimate, the penetration is marvelously deep.

"Damn, Ava, you feel so fucking good!"

"I love how you feel too, baby!"

"Oh, baby. I love fucking you."

"I love the way you fuck me, it's so good."

As our bodies bounce in rhythm, we grow silent. I love the quiet sound of sex. The panting, the skin on skin smacking, no words. No oh baby, fuck me. Just the smooth rhythm of flesh on flesh.

We move our fuckfest into the bedroom and soon collapse on the bed out of breath.

"Man, you are so freaky! I love that about you. I've never been with anyone so wild and free and so damn hot! We do need to work on your rhythm, though. Are you ready for some more of this?"

"Sure."

What in the hell is wrong with my rhythm? He's always telling me I'm not in rhythm, but also that I'm so good at sex. Such a contradiction.

I move to position myself to perform oral sex on Dan in the bed. As he moans and groans with excitement, I begin to cry, but he doesn't notice. I desperately want something better for myself. The sex is amazing, but also extremely lonely. I know this isn't a real relationship.

We finish for a second time and I move to get up from the bed.

"Well, I'd better get going."

"You don't want some more of this?"

No, and it's not good for my self-esteem anyway.

"Of course, but I drove today instead of taking the Metro, and the parking garage closes at eleven, and I've got to get back to the dogs."

"You and those damn dogs. You know you need to move into the city so we can spend more time together. I don't know why you live out in the middle of nowhere."

"I only live five miles away on the other side of the Potomac. And if you came to see me, then parking wouldn't be an issue."

"True, and I do come your way sometimes, but since you were here tonight anyway this made sense."

"It did, but I've got to go now. I had the dog walker come and feed the dogs dinner, but I still need to get back to them."

"Yeah, never mind my needs."

"You know, I'm sure here in the DMV you could find someone who is dog-free that can be here at your beck and call. If you don't already have a side check, that is."

"I don't want another woman. You know you are the only one I can trust. And you and I just fit well together. We have great chemistry. So, how did your meeting go?"

"What meeting?"

"I thought you were here in the city to have a meeting?"

"I guess if you call a therapy session a meeting."

"Do you really think you need therapy?"

"I do, and I think you do too, but that's on you to figure out."

"You are crazy."

"Well, then it's a good thing I'm in therapy."

"You know what I mean. So, what's your issue?"

"You."

"Me?"

"I need to get you out of my life and yet here I am, with you again. This thing we do is going nowhere. You want to act like we're a couple, but as soon as you get too close, you shut down and walk out of my life and don't speak to me for months, and then you show up again and I take you back, and the craziness repeats for another cycle."

"You really are crazy. I have told you I don't want to be in a relationship."

"And I have told you, neither do I, but whatever this weird ass thing we're doing is not working. You accuse me of getting too close or trying to have your baby. Really I think you have commitment issues, but again that's on you to seek help for. I'm just tried of riding the roller coaster of crazy with you."

"You say this every time and every time you still give me head and let me have my way with you."

"Exactly why I'm in therapy. Goodnight."

"You know I'm not going to let you walk to your car alone, so stop with the attitude, at least until you get home. Come on."

We head out of his condo to the elevator.

"So, did you see the special report analyzing the State of the Union address from earlier this year?"

"Yeah, it was interesting, but I'm still concerned about the president's foreign policy issues."

"Yeah, I hear you, but his immigration reform is on point."

"True. I am hopeful that his ideas are put into law."

We enter the elevator and Dan leans over to give me a hug.

"You know I have issues right?"

"You've explained a lot to me about your past over the last few years, so, yeah, I know."

"So, how's work?"

"It still sucks."

"Yeah, I hear you. I don't know how much longer I can take working on The Hill. I'm ready to quit and move to an island somewhere. You can come with me and be my sex toy."

"That is not even remotely tempting."

"You know you'd love it."

We exit the elevator and walk outside. We cross the street to the parking garage and head to my car. We get in and I begin driving out of the garage as Dan rests his head on my shoulder. Once we are at the gate I stop to let him out.

"Goodnight."

He kisses me on the lips.

"Goodnight. Call me when you get home."

"Okay."

Dan exits the car and stands to the side as I drive off.

This is the longest shortest drive. I have a million thoughts running through my head every time I leave Dan's, like, why in the hell do I go over there? Why can't I get it through my broken heart that he's never going to commit to a relationship with me? And why can't I open my heart to love someone who will?

I'm glad to be home and be with my girls who love me unconditionally.

"Hello, my baby girls! How was your day?"

I walk to the back door to let the dogs outside, and send Dan a text: *Made it home. Had a great time.*

He replies: *Me too. Sweet dreams.*

We return inside and I give them a treat. It's now time for my bath. Every night this scalding hot water, which discolors my legs, is my retreat. It's in this lobster boiling water that I let go of it all; thoughts and feelings fade. By the time I get out I am so exhausted I collapse on the bed and then pass out for the night. I've never taken drugs, but this feels like my fix.

7

Back at Shawshank

~

I am at my desk when Col Baker seems to appear out of nowhere.

"Ava! Happy Hump Day!"

"Same to you, sir."

"Ava, I need you to take this meeting in an hour. It's with OSD, Joint Staff, and the State Department. It's regarding our latest partnership agreements. Oh, and there's a budget meeting I need you to sit in on this afternoon. I know that's not in our job jar, but, well, it kind of sort of is anyway, and you've got a budget background."

"Sure thing, sir. Are there read-aheads for these meetings?"

"Lieutenant Colonel Davis should have something for both. I may have some emails, but I probably deleted them."

"Oh?"

"Yeah, I don't bother with read-aheads anymore. Really, what's the point, right? Same thing, different day, different meeting. Just show up and try not to fall asleep and occasionally make some random point and you're good to go."

"Never thought of it that way."

As Colonel Baker walks off, I check my email and see I have a message from Marcy:

Need updates for SecDef's meeting ASAP. He returns in two days and we will need to brief him on Project X.

I need a coffee break.

I leave my desk and walk out of the office. I enter a convenience store at the end of the hall and make a cup of coffee and then stare at the pastry shelf. I grab a huge muffin and head to the cashier. Waiting in line I see the lottery scratch offs. Maybe today's my lucky day—but it never is. I try to be in a great, positive mood before I scratch off the number, but so far, no luck. I think I'll pass on the lottery today, although it would be cool to hear about a Pentagon employee winning. I bet a lot of people have no clue you can buy lottery tickets in here. Powerball, Mega Millions, and scratch-offs are how some seem to make it through the day. I always feel a little embarrassed when I ask for a ticket, but there are some who have no shame and announce proudly how many they want, and whether they want a quick pick or have a list of numbers they're betting on. Since, in all this time I've never heard of anyone in this building winning anything big, I would say there are a lot of disappointed people roaming these corridors, or perhaps, very hopeful people. I don't know. I just know I fucking hate my job.

I'M NOW SITTING in a conference room with thirty other people, military and civilian. There are also people on the video teleconference. Marcy is heading the meeting. Marcy dresses like a hippie, and I'm not sure why this is acceptable for someone who works in OSD. She's about 5'5", has long brown hair, and is super pale, with green eyes. Today she's wearing some long flower skirt and a hot pink sweater that looks like it needs be to be thrown in the trash. Let me come to work like that and they'd put me a corner for sure, but that's just one of the differences between the races here at Shawshank.

"Thank you all for joining us this morning."

Why, oh, why do I have to be here for this?

"As you all know, last week we ended with needing to have another meeting, so today we are going to go over the discussion from last week to see if we can reach a resolution this week. In the event that we do not reach a consensus, I have taken the liberty to schedule another meeting for next week. Let's get started, shall we?"

As Marcy continues the meeting, I begin to think about revisions to my children's book. Maybe I should have Cleo and Sophie sing a special song before they take off for their adventures. Yes! That's something children will love and it makes it more unique. I begin to take notes about the revisions and then begin to write out a grocery list. I always wait until my cupboards are bare, so I really don't need a list; pretty much, I just shop on every aisle in the store.

"Looks like we'll need to meet again on this issue. Next meeting is already scheduled for next Wednesday. Thank you."

I get up and catch the smile of Frank.

"Boy, you sure do take a lot of notes in these meetings. I never do, but my boss never asks about them either, so there's that."

"My boss doesn't care either, but honestly, fifty percent of my notes are on another subject. Sitting here for an hour allows me time to work out other issues."

"I hadn't thought of that. I should try that; two birds, one stone."

"More like ten birds, one stone. See you later."

"See you."

8
Salon Night

~

I love the salon. It's where I can let go, vent about anything, and be black for a few hours, although, like I said, there are some in the Pentagon who stay black most of the day. I'm different, and I view those folks as ghetto and simple. Bougie, I know.

I'm reading a magazine when Monique, my stylist, calls me to her chair.

"Monique, what's up?"

"Same, same. What's up with you?"

"Same and needing a change."

"What kind of a change?"

"A job change."

"Girl! You know you ain't going to do any better than working at the Pentagon!"

"I can't allow myself to believe that."

"Well, what do you want to be doing?"

"I want to be a writer. I'm working on a children's book series now."

"A writer! Girl, how you going to go from Top Secret shit to Bambi? You messing with me, right?"

"No, I'm serious. I love to write and I've been writing since I was seven years old."

"Girl, what?"

"Yeah, one night I wrote a little story and made illustrations and everything. I took it to school the next day and my teacher loved it. She laminated it and bound it with yarn and read it to the class. I was so proud!"

"What was it about?"

"Okay, don't laugh, but it was called, "The Boy Who Loved the Color, Lime" and everything he had was lime, from his room to his dog."

"Lime, huh? Not green? You were an advanced little bougie something!"

"Go on and laugh, but it was a masterpiece!"

"Girl, I'm done with you! But that's impressive, though. Look, I'm all about following your passion. I did it, so I say, go for it."

"So, what was there before hair?"

"Can you believe I was an engineer?"

"Really? And you wonder how I can go from Top Secret to Bambi?"

"Yeah, cause most folks don't go that far right, but I guess you and me are the different ones."

"How did you make the change?"

"I just decided I had to start living for me. But it wasn't easy."

"Yeah, I can imagine."

"Yeah, I had to make sure I had a good solid plan in place."

"You mean, like having a good savings built up first?"

"Partially, but I mean a guaranteed way that I wouldn't falter. I had to build it."

"Okay, I'm lost."

Monique looks around to see no one is within earshot before speaking.

"Before I just up and quit my job, I designed a device that would allow me to switch on and off the left and right sides of my brain."

"Wait, what?"

"I created a device that allows me to stay in right-brain mode so I could pursue my passion. Sometimes I switch over to the left-brain when I'm doing the Monique-shop-owner thing, but otherwise I stay in right-brain mode. Without it, I would have been begging for my old job back within a month."

"So, now, what? Don't you need your left brain for cosmetology school? And where is it and how does it work?"

"The computer is in my head and the switch is right here on my wrist. I did need my left brain for school, but that was the only time I switched over during the transition. And only for a few hours a day, max."

I notice two small bumps on Monique's right wrist.

"Monique, it's only Wednesday, but I must be exhausted already because I can't believe this is a real conversation we're having."

"Oh, it's real. I can hook you up with one to test it out. You can see how it works for you before you quit."

"I don't know if I could ever be brave like you and quit, but it does sound like something that could help me not hate my job as much, right? Like I switch to left-brain just before I get to work and then over to right-brain for the rest of the day. I could then tolerate my job and write like crazy while I am at home!"

"You can try it that way, but I guarantee you, after a while it's going to give you the balls to say, 'Fuck you, bitches, I'm doing my Bambi shit full-time'!"

"So, basically, I'll have a Stepford chip."

"What now?"

"You know, like the movie, *The Stepford Wives*. The seventies version, though; I didn't like the remake."

"Oh, yeah, I feel you! I hadn't thought of it like that, but yeah! I'll tell you what. I'll give you a call in about a week and we'll get this thing going."

"Is it going to hurt?"

"Hell, yeah. Girl, no. Okay, not really. Seriously, no more than getting a tattoo. And, I do it like outpatient surgery with a local anesthetic and there's no recovery time. Oh, and we'll have to add some tracks to cover the scar."

"Okay, how much is this going to cost me? And why am I one hundred percent okay with this idea?"

"'Cause you ready for that change. You'll be like my test case since it's hard to test the device on myself. All you need to do is bring the hair for your extensions 'cause you know you be all fancy with your five-hundred-dollar weave!"

"Whatever! Since I'm getting a new look in a few days, how about just a wash and style tonight."

"That will work. So, how's your man?"

"I keep going to therapy to leave him, but I haven't yet."

"Therapy? Girl, you and your therapy. You know how you can leave him?"

"How?"

"Just leave his ass! I'm serious. It's going to hurt and you'll feel like, damn, maybe I made a mistake, and then he'll call trying to get back in your bed and you'll let him 'cause you'll be all horny and whatnot and then he's going to say or do something jackass-ish like he always does and this time you're going to look at him and say get the fuck out. And the sex sucked anyway."

"Really? You think I haven't tried this before?"

"I think you have, but you've messed up the exit strategy. The key is to do it right at the point when you just got laid and right when he's an ass. I'm guessing this has occurred before but you just let it slide 'cause you just got some good stuff and you were feeling all connected to him and shit, but what I'm saying is, be ready to get a good lay and be mentally ready to lay without him that night 'cause you kicked his ass out."

"I hear you. I'll have to get ready for that, though."

"You want me to play some 'Rocky' for you?"

"'Rocky'? Like the movie?"

"Girl, yes. That's my go-to music whenever I need to get pumped up. It's more than just the theme song, you know. There's a bunch of them from every movie."

"True! I'm a diehard *Rocky* fan, so I know, but I only use them to push through my runs."

"Well, now you can use them to push that ass out of your life!"

8
Thursday

~

Same shit.

9

Fridays

~

I love Fridays in the building. These days bring the most ceremonies for promotions and retirements. What's most amusing about them is most of them take place in "the hallway," for lack of a better way to describe it. We have large areas between the corridors, technically called "apexes," that can seat about fifty people, and there you go, a room for a celebration. They can be disruptive, though, with women's heels clacking, the custodian rolling the trash bin down the hall, etc. While most do try to be quiet and polite, the noise is just there, but those in the honoree role seem unaffected. It's their day. Family, friends, co-workers, and high-ranking officers all come to support the event. The retirements seem the most enjoyable to me. Whether I'm attending one or just trying to quietly tiptoe past one, I can feel the excitement, and the joy of ending an accomplished military career.

In the building you see them all—Army, Navy, Air Force, and Marines—but the vibe for each is still the same. I don't see many civilian retirements, and we only have ceremonies for promotion to SES, although once in Oklahoma I attended a GS-15 (the step before SES) pinning ceremony. It was interesting, I thought, but I wasn't moved. We civilians give a lot. And, we take a lot of crap from the Military, especially here at Shawshank. This is their house, their headquarters. But we don't deploy unless we want to (for the most part, although I do think there are some exceptions for special skills); we don't leave our families for months or a year, or have back-to-back deployments like we saw with the last two wars. We don't end our careers thanking our spouses for raising our kids because we were hardly around. We don't pick up and move that often; only the true go-getter civilians or those wanting an escape like me have any mobility under their belt.

Of course when I complain that as a federal employee I can't get my full pension until I have served forty years, my dad reminds me that I chose my uniform, and he is right. I could be heading out the door next year if I had been in the military, but I don't wear Blues or ABUs or a flight suit. I wear super cute business suits and four-inch heels. My dad's a Vet, but never encouraged my sister and me to join the Service. I've never asked him why, but I'm sure there's a good reason. Maybe it's like Furious says in the movie *Boyz in the Hood*—a black man ain't got no place in the Army. Most days I'm certain a black *woman* ain't got no place in the Pentagon.

In either case they mostly all come back. The double dippers. What's the point of retiring from the military only to come back a couple of months later, wearing a suit like me? Are times so bad that everyone has to keep working after their military career? And not a fun, get-me-out-of-the-house job, but a full-up, six-figure job. Since most of them don't do much either before or after they return as a civilian, I guess it makes sense. Come here, make about $150,000 and not do much but have coffee and close out a bunch of taskers, or get a minimum-wage gig just to get out of the house; both get you human interaction, but one pays a hell of a lot more.

I think, though, I am most disturbed by those who retire as colonials and come back as SESs. I have to think for the most part if you could have made general officer (GO) you would have stayed in—although there are some exceptions to that thought—but if you couldn't get promoted to GO, why are you back as a GO equivalent? And what about me? That's supposed to be *my* path to the top and you jumped out of your lane and found your way into mine. Not only *in* my lane, but way the hell ahead of me. *And* you suck. You are not a good leader. You are not someone who should be an SES, which is why I'm sure you didn't make GO.

And so the game is played: favoritism and nepotism is real in the DoD. But why? If people know you suck, why do they bring you back? How do we ever get better as a defense department if we just keep inbreeding? I don't doubt being a full-time writer will be challenging, and unless I own a publishing company, too, I will have to answer to someone (although there's the option of self-publishing). But I would rather deal with foolish shit and be doing what I love than deal with foolish shit in a job I hate. Yet, I'm still here.

Gotta write more and get my shit published.

10

Happy Hour

~

Thank you, God, it's Friday night, and tonight is Happy Hour with the girls.

I'm running late, but I roll with the world's most habitually late women who take CP (Colored People) time to a whole new level, so it should be all good. I enjoy their company and I wish we could do it more often, except that I am rarely in the mood to hang out. I wonder why? When I am about to do something or have just done something fun, I'm all about, "I should do this more often," but not even twenty-four hours later, I couldn't imagine going through the effort to go out again in the near future. I'm pretty sure it's some form of depression, but I've not mentioned it in therapy. I've got enough to deal with. I see Terry and Dana at the bar. Terry is waving like she's signaling for help on the side of the road. I'm not sure why, since I am looking at her square in the face.

"Ava, girl! Over here!"

"Hey! How is everyone?"

"Enjoying a long overdue happy hour. And you are late, Missy," Dana scolds.

I give her the look. The "you know damn well why I'm late" look.

"I had a last-minute tasker to work."

"Don't you hate those? They are never about anything. Hell, nothing is ever about anything, but yet it's got to be done right now!"

"I don't think we'd know how to act if everything wasn't a fire."

"I would and I do. You and Terry are way too dedicated. I just do my time and go home. Heck, I was here early!"

"I can tell. You're pretty lit."

"Oh, yeah, she's lit alright!" Jamie joins us. "Hey, y'all! What did I miss?"

Terry rolls her eyes. "Happy hour."

"Terry, why you got to be so bitchy? Now come on, y'all still here, and Ava, I know, just got here 'cause she ain't got no drink in her hand."

"I know why I'm late, but what about you?"

"I got stopped in the hall by our 2-star," I explain, glad to have the chance to decompress and say this out loud. "He wanted me to back-brief him on a meeting from this morning. But of course that led to why don't I send him a one-pager, which he just had to read over the weekend. Never mind I'm headed out of the office with my purse on my shoulder."

Dana smacks her lips.

"You're just as whacked out as these two. You know, you *can* say, 'I'm leaving for the day, and I will get that for you first thing Monday.' I mean, really, what is he going to do? Fire you? You's one of them gov'ment employees, it'll take him years to try to fire you, and while he's doing that, you can sue for discrimination or some shit. And neither of you got time for any of that shit.

"I know, but I just don't know how to say no."

"I do. You know none of us are getting promoted anytime soon, so who needs all this facetime? Girl, I would have looked at him and said, 'Hell no, peace out'! Seriously, it's so hard to fire a federal employee that by the time they did, you'd be ready to retire anyway." (Funny, I was just living out this scenario earlier this week.)

Jamie is shaking her head and checking her phone. She's been dating some new guy, so I'm guessing she's hoping to see a text or missed call from him, but she says, distracted, "You don't ever get moved to just be all you can be?"

"Honey, this is no old school Army commercial, and I work for the Navy anyhow! Speaking of which, where is Sheryl?"

I point to her at the front of the bar.

"She's here. I saw her when I came in. She was flirting with some man. He was super cute."

"Is he a congressman, senator, or a lowly staffer? You know she's all about snagging her a Capitol Hill man."

I pause for a second, thinking.

"You know, with all the men in the Pentagon, it's odd how we've never click with anyone. Why do you think that is, Ms. Dana?"

"I don't think it's odd. Those men are crazy or just trying to have affairs, and I am not trying to be anyone's side chick!"

"I guess, but it sure would be nice. But yeah, every guy that has ever approached me in that building has been 'special,' and not in a good way. Anyway, I'm ready for the one."

Jamie pretends to choke on her drink.

"Girl, stop! I thought you had the one. Mr. Superfine from Capitol Hill. Sheryl over there is trying to get what you got. Are you saying you don't want it anymore?"

"I'm saying I want a real relationship, not meaningless sex with a commitment-phobe."

"Yes, how tragic for you. You get Mr. Superfine hot sex and we get nothing."

"I'd take nothing over this shit."

Terry stares me down before she begins her standard lines about Dan.

"I wish I could kick his ass! He's such a jerk to you."

"Nope. I'm a jerk to me. I keep falling for his 'us' and 'we' and 'our' and 'let's make babies' bullshit, and then he's like, oh no, you are trying to marry me and have my baby. I think he might be bi-polar."

Jamie spits out part of her drink.

"Ava, really?"

"Really, I'm not joking. It's kind of crazy what he does, and it's exhausting."

"Maybe you two should try therapy."

"Ha! Dan would never go to therapy, though he is very supportive of me going because clearly I need it and not His Greatness."

Terry gives me the serious stare again.

"You really should drop his ass."

Saved by Sheryl. And I have got to stop bringing up Dan. I think I do it to get a good kick in the ass from my friends like Terry, but then I never leave him, and I end up just looking weak.

"Ladies! What have I missed?"

Sheryl bounces into our group smiling and waving. She must have done well with the gentleman she was with. As for him, I'd think it's hard for any man not to think he's scored well with her. She's poised, intelligent, always decked out in a killer business suit (skirts only—must show her slender mocha legs). She's a natural beauty; barely wears more than a light foundation and lip gloss. Her hair is always shiny, and her eyes sparkle as if she's got Christmas lights behind those dark brown things.

Dana turns her back to Sheryl. "Really?"

"Really! I tried to say hello when you came in, but you didn't see me."

Dana turns around to face Sheryl. "So, whose number did you get tonight?"

"His name is Michael, and he's a lawyer."

"Nice."

"Isn't it, though. Next round on me!"

Terry signals the bartender. "Works for me! Well, now that we're Purple let's have some fun!" She means that purple is the color that represents the Joint Staff, a big happy family of Army, Navy, Air Force, and Marines.

Jamie now seems confused. "Wait, what about our bitching session?"

Terry throws her hands up. "Can we for once skip the 'I hate my good-paying, I don't know what else I'd be doing if I didn't have it' government job rant?"

"No, 'cause I need to get this off my chest," says Jamie. "Do you know that I've been assigned to a new acquisition program?"

Terry scratches her head. "Are we supposed to be shocked or upset or something?"

"I was knee-deep in what I was already assigned to, the new radar, and now I need to formulate a team to look at acquiring a new sensor."

Terry is slowing sipping her drink as she stares at Jamie, "Either I'm confused or just don't care. Jamie, your job is to do your job, whatever it is these people give you to do."

"I know that, but I'm tired of being shifted around from one thing to the next with the excuse, 'you're our best, so we need you to lead this effort.'"

"Yeah, 'cause that's insulting."

"It is when everyone around me is getting promoted and I'm not, but somehow I'm the best."

Dana breaks out into a smile as she gives Jamie a hug. "Like I was saying earlier, only do the minimum and take your ass home."

"You make it sound so simple."

"'Cause it is so damn simple. You bitches all stressed out and graying out and for what? A paycheck that you're going to get anyway?"

I notice Sheryl nodding her head, and she comes with it: "I'm with you, but one must have the mindset of laziness to collect a check for not working."

Here we go. Dana is pissed at this statement.

"Oh, I'm not lazy, honey. I'm smart. Every day I get up, dress in one of my nice suits and show up. I am prepared for anything they throw at me and always have my leadership prepared for their meetings. But when the clock strikes 4 PM, I have purse on shoulder and hand on door. And ain't nobody stopping me on my way out asking for shit. That's giving it all and no more."

Sheryl is pissed. "You sound like a secretary; not a high-level government employee."

"And? Does it really matter what you do as long as you can pay your bills and have a nice life? Y'all be wanting too much. This is not Corporate America. This is welfare masked as a job, thus requiring you get your ass up and go to work each day."

Terry smiles. "Welfare, nice."

Dana smirks as she takes a sip of her drink. "Welfare, federal employment; one in the same."

Sheryl is about to lose it. "That is such a Republican thing to say. You know, if you had any concern about the DoD mission, you'd feel differently."

It's time for me to chime in. "Probably not."

Dana reaches to give me a high-five. "Thank you!"

"You think what we do is for naught, and I think that as well, only I just don't know how to turn off my concern like you. If I could, I'm sure I too could see this as glorified welfare."

Jamie finds her way into the middle of our group as she over-exaggerates a pout.

"Somehow we got off the subject of me and my issue?"

Dana looks confused. "Really?"

"Whatever, Dana. I was serious about my issues."

Sheryl clears her throat. "Does anyone have anything planed for the weekend?"

I am happy to announce that I do. "Marva and I are going to our pole fitness class tomorrow."

"Nice! Soon you'll be able to work that pole for Dan!"

"Sure."

Terry shouts, "Drop his ass, Ava!" which causes those around us to glance our way and then write us off as loud black women.

Sheryl, very confused, asks, "What am I missing here?"

Jamie provides the background. "Nothing. Same thing, different month. Right?"

And I concur. "Yep. So, let's not go there, and let's hear about Mr. Lawyer instead."

Jamie starts to pout again. "Are we really ignoring my issue?"

Terry reaches over to give Jamie a hug. "Yes, honey, we are," she says, as she signals for the waiter. "Let's get this round Sheryl's buying."

11

Pole Fitness

~

I never drink until I'm drunk because I believe I'm too old for that sort of thing, but I did get a good buzz going last night. I really needed it. Terry was good to get us together for some downtime; plus, it's our safe place, a place where we can be as black as we want to be. At Shawshank we must conform and tuck that shit away for ten or more hours a day… well, except for the Steve Harvey 1990s suit crew.

This morning is going to be good. I'm heading to the Metro to meet Marva for the pole fitness class. It's rather funny since I have absolutely no rhythm, but I get in that studio and change into my stripper heels and let loose for an hour; and, any amount of time with Marva is special. She's my spiritual guide. There have been so many times when I've had something on my mind, and then out of the blue Marva calls me at work. She starts talking about something and then bam, she's Iyanla Vanzant-ing some truth that I needed to hear without ever knowing what's been on my mind. I've told her she's my angel, and she just smiles.

As I approach the platform, I see Marva. She's always happy and smiling. She's short like me and has a body I'd love to call my own. She's a petite black Barbie. She's a beautiful brown caramel-colored woman who rocks a silk press Chinese bob.

"Hey! Sorry you couldn't make happy hour last night."

"Girl, you know I can't deal with that crew when they're all liquored up."

"Actually, last night wasn't so bad. More talking than drinking, but you didn't miss anything."

"I know I didn't. I was at home watching *The Color Purple*."

"Why?"

"The question is, why not? I never, ever get tired of that movie. And, it serves as a reminder to not settle for anything, but to keep pushing to get to where you agreed with God you'd be in this life."

Before I can ask Marva to elaborate, the train arrives. We step in and take a seat and as always, she knows I want to know more, so she continues.

"I believe we all have these conversations with God before we are born; well, our souls do, that is, and it's then that we know what family we will be born into and what we are to accomplish during this lifetime."

I'm smiling at Marva, which makes her give me a laugh.

"You think I'm crazy, right?"

"Not at all. I was just thinking about this myself; well, not to that level, but the thought that we are born with a purpose that's buried in us. I just can't figure out what mine is and how to go about figuring it out."

"No need. God will reveal it all to you when then time is right."

"Indeed, He will."

As the train reaches our stop, we stand up and hold on to the back of the seat. We are both in a happy place, as this pole fitness class serves as a stress release for both of us. We exit the train and head out of the station. It's not quite fall, but this morning the air is crisp which causes us to walk with a little pep in our step. As we begin walking to the studio, which is a few blocks from the Metro station, we are silent. Marva, who is about ten years older than me, is worldly wise and yet, optimistic. I say those as a contrast because, to me, they are. How can you become be so knowing and still have any level of hope about anything?

"So, how's that wonderful man of yours?"

Thank goodness we are just a few feet away from the studio. I won't have to lie to Marva for very long. I don't have the heart to tell her Dan's an ass. Or, maybe I'm just too embarrassed. Marva thinks I'm steadily growing into this great person with this higher spiritual level of understanding and yet, on a weekly basis, I endure face fucking and one style of sex with Dan, the asshole. She thinks we're perfect, and I can't stand the thought of us actually not being that way, so I lie to her. Fortunately our other friends don't talk about men around Marva since she is more "religious"; none of them will ever know that, for Marva, I have painted my relationship with Dan to be this magical fairy tale.

"He's doing great. Do you ever think of what the folks at your church would say if they knew you came here? I think the people at mine would stop speaking to me."

"No, I've never thought about it. To me it's exercise and it shouldn't really matter how you stay in shape just as long as you do. But, yes, I think if I ever mentioned it, I would be, first, the most sought-after person by our single men folk, and then, shunned by the women. Some folks can be so uptight."

We enter the studio and head for the changing room. As we are shedding jackets and sweatpants we see her: the super tall chick who we have both decided is using this class to get a job at a strip club. Every week by the end of class we find her at the top of the pole sliding down like a wet noodle. The rest of us are barely able to do a kick, wrap, and swirl, but she has somehow hoisted herself up to the ceiling like a cat and is slowly and seductively working her way back down. Oh well, at least I look good in my stripper shoes. I once wore them when Dan came over, but he wasn't moved. I really don't get that man at all.

Did I mention I have a love/hate relationship with this class? Love the workout; hate the fact that I have no rhythm or coordination. The hour is long and frustrating, but fun because I'm with Marva. I think I keep coming back because I have this need to master everything, which is a result of low self-esteem, which is the result of having parents who didn't give a shit about me, which has resulted in me having Dan in my life. In any case, I'm back for another week of this, so here goes. This week's goal: hoist myself up to the top of the pole and seductively slide down. So far I've failed at this, even with the sticky powder stuff they give you to keep a grip on the pole. Well, if I fail again this week, I'm sure to still get in a good workout and be sore as hell for the next two days.

I also feel a sense of improved self-esteem. I think that these sexy moves, no matter how awkward I may look doing them, make me ready for Dan. Get me closer to having this rhythm he keeps complaining about. He says we're not in rhythm when we fuck. I've never been told this before, but maybe that's because I have mostly been with white men. I've only had sex with two black men before Dan. With one, I lost my virginity and was date raped, and the other was a drug addict car salesman who I dated when I first moved to Oklahoma. I got pregnant by him, too. I was three months out of college and pregnant by a man I didn't know. I didn't find out until about a year later he was crackhead. I've always used this, though, as a good reason why having an abortion was the best decision. First, I would have risked having a baby with issues because of the drugs in his system, and second, I would have had a crackhead as a baby daddy and that would have been equally as bad for the child.

Again I digress. I see Marva is thoroughly enjoying today's class as she's freaking the heck out of her pole. Maybe I'll sign up for the chair dancing class. I think that's more my speed.

"Ava, girl, you have got to be in the present moment, honey."

"Yeah, I know. That would at least keep me on beat, 'cause you know I have no rhythm."

"Honey, everyone's got rhythm. You just got to be right here, right now, and feel it!"

"Okay." I give Marva a weak smile as we head to the changing room.

"So, what's up after this?"

"Nothing today. Just going back home to hang with my dogs."

"Sounds like something to me."

We're heading out of the studio and I'm dying to ask Marva a question. I know she will have the right answer. She always does.

"You know when you told me that you can sense when your mom's soul is in your presence?"

"Yes, of course. I smell the perfume she used to wear. Why? Have you had a visitor?"

"I think so. I think it's my grandmother, only she doesn't come with a scent."

Marva is doing all she can to not burst out laughing.

"Go ahead and laugh!"

"No. Nope. Not laughing at you. I'm just finding it hard to contain my excitement! I knew you were blessed, gifted, that is."

"Well, okay, I guess. But for me, it's when I'm walking my dogs in the park. I get a strong sensation and I can't stop thinking about her and then a pile of leaves will whirl around in front of me. I think that's her."

"You think she's the wind?"

"No, not the wind, but that she has the power to move those leaves and let me know she's with me."

"Oh, well then, yes, most definitely."

"I miss her so much, even though I never really knew her."

"Sounds like you're carrying some guilt."

"I am. I really am. By the time I started to spend time with her she was already becoming forgetful. She knew me, but then a few years later she got worse. She still knew me, but she was different. She knew my dad and she knew me, but she lost the connection that I was his daughter. It was very strange for me to witness. How did she know he was her son and I was her granddaughter, but forgot I was his daughter? Whose daughter did she think I was? Crazy, I know, trying to get into the mind of a person who had dementia."

"I think you're trying to hold on to the memories of someone whose presence is with you all the time. Just enjoy her as she is now. I know it's strange. You can't see her and hug her, but she's here. You'll be amazed at how connected you can be with the soul."

We've reached the Metro and are just in time to hop on the train.

"Thanks, Marva. You know everything."

"No, but I feel like I've been through about everything."

12

Zenful Sundays

~

It's our spot. The bank on the river is the peaceful place where Cleo, Sophie and I relax after a nice nature walk on Mount Vernon Trail. For us, it's our weekly mini-vacation. It's where we unwind after a long week of work, playing fetch and tummy rubs. Sometimes we are there for hours in this tranquil state of being. It is there where I know all is well in our world.

It's most definitely a Dan-free zone. I couldn't get him out here if I tried, but that's perfectly fine with me. This is our time. We've been through a lot, the three of us, and while some was good, some memories are very sad. But these two little troopers have been there for me. They are my light and my laugh. They are my friends and my confidantes, my snuggle-buddies and alarm clocks! Without them I wouldn't know how to let loose, how to unwind. With them I am free to be me. They never laugh at my dancing to music or singing off-key, though I think if they could speak, the sweet little looks on their faces would say, "Mommy, please! You are so silly!"

I am a better person because of Cleo and Sophie. I am stronger, happier, freer, and humbler. I am alive. If only, though, this feeling could last past Sunday afternoons. I wonder how I can make that happen? I can't feel Zenful five days of the week because Shawshank is anything but Zen. I can't when I leave a therapy session feeling better about life, but then do an about face, and end the night in Dan's bed being criticized for not having sexual rhythm. How can I be Zenful when my dream is to be a successful writer and so far all I've done throughout my life is dabble at it?

PART II

{CHANGES}

13

Monday, Again

~

My heart bleeds for the protesters outside the building. Maybe not "bleeds," but you've got to give them their props. They have a cause and passion and they stick with it. Granted, I want to tell them they are wasting their time, as they are protesting at the Metro entrance, which is not the place to get into the minds of the policy makers in DoD. Here at the Metro entrance, you will find us, the regular people. Yes, you will see the military, but they are mostly colonels and below, and they don't have the power to change anything. We, the regular people, believe in the mission; we come, we serve, and we go home. I guess, though, the protesters aren't allowed on the other side of the building. The side with the black SUVs and people who still can't really make a difference, but do sit in the highest positions within the Defense Department.

Matters not. It's Monday and my groundhog week begins again.

I've been at work for about an hour, and so far, same old same old. But since it's getting time for our staff meeting, I'll get some good comic relief for the day. I get up from my desk and enter our makeshift conference room. Col Baker is already seated at a small table with a handful of people from our office.

"Okay, guys, here are the notes from my staff meeting with the boss. Oh, but first, how was everyone's weekend? Anyone have any great stories to share?"

The group gives a collective no.

"You guys need to live it up more! This weekend I went to a new golf course and it was a challenge, I'll tell you. Really? Nothing fun from any of you? Okay, let's go through these notes. Al, the general is wanting an update on your aircraft fleet stuff."

"Yes, sir, I'll schedule time on his calendar. You know, we've been on his calendar twice now, and both times he canceled the meeting, but not because he has a conflict."

"Yeah, that's a bummer. Just try again. He's probably just blowing you off since it's pretty clear he's not interested, but he asked for it again, so try again."

"Okay, sir."

"Ava, he wants to know if you've been able to kill that All Call thing."

"No, sir. It's still scheduled for Wednesday."

"Really?"

(Why would I really say it was if it wasn't?)

"Yes, sir. A group calendar invite went out last week. Major General Deeds should have it on his calendar as well, but I will check."

"Wow, yeah, I guess no one noticed it, not even his Exec. How does that happen?" (Because no one gives a fuck about what goes one around here.)

"I'm not sure, sir, but I will look into it."

"Do we have slides for this thing?"

"No, I thought I'd just let him wing it. It's good practice for him."

"Oh, okay."

(There should be great concern that this man actually believes me right now. Why wouldn't I have thought to have slides for a 3-star's meeting? Why do people ask the most ridiculous questions?)

"I'm kidding, sir. I emailed them to you last week and you replied with an okay, so I sent them on for Lieutenant General Green's use."

"I'll be damned. Last week must have been crazy because I don't recall any of this."

"Yes, sir, it must have been."

(If busy means not doing anything yourself and sending me to all your meetings.)

"Mike, how's that policy memo coming?"

My phone is ringing, thank goodness, and I get up to answer it.

"Hey, Steve, we're having our staff meeting. What's up?"

"Hey, I just saw that All Call on the calendar. I didn't want you to spend the morning wasting your time. Sorry I overlooked it."

"No worries, and thanks. You just saved me a morning of running around."

"Yeah, now you are free to run around on something else that is just as not important."

"Ha! Talk to you later. Thanks."

"Later."

I return to the staff meeting to see a frustrated Col Baker.

"Don't tell me we have some short suspense?" (Unlike a regular suspense, these tend to have far less flexibility on the due date, and are in fact due within hours or a day, but that never stops us from an attempted negotiation.)

"No, sir. It was just Steve letting me know he found the All Call on the calendar."

"Great. Why are we having it again?"

(Kill me NOW!)

"To hand out the overdue quarterly awards and for Lieutenant General Green to better articulate his project."

"Yes, that's right. And you couldn't talk him out of that?"

(And...Groundhog Day before noon; we're breaking records today!)

"No, sir. I did see him last week in our planning meeting and I did mention it, but I was unsuccessful in convincing him to turn off this meeting."

"Ava, you've finally been defeated. I never thought I'd see the day. But this just makes you one to a gazillion, so you're still on the plus side. Not a lot of folks at your level who have the boss's ear."

"Yes, sir. Oh, sir, also I need to mention that Policy will be sending a set of MOAs (Memorandums of Agreement) for review. They are for several countries we are partnering with."

"Sure. Does it need to be seen by Lieutenant General Green?"

"Yes, sir. These will have to be approved by the Chief, actually, since they will be signed by the SecDef."

"Okay, well, I guess you can look them over for me and shoot them up to Major General Deeds to coord on."

"Sure thing, sir."

(Lowest grade, lowest pay, all the shit.)

"Great! Around the room. Anything? Still no fun stories about your weekends? You guys are so boring!"

14

The Implantation

~

Somehow with the fairly smart mind I have and the master's degree to boot, I have still decided to have my hairdresser cut open my head tonight and implant some thingamabob that she has invented in my brain. I am certain I should have driven myself to a mental institution instead, but here I sit in Monique's basement, looking around at her makeshift operating table and seemingly sterile equipment.

"I'm pretty sure I'm not supposed to be this calm right now."

"I don't know why you would be anything but calm. Well, maybe excited, too, but if you're waiting to freak out, that's not going to happen."

"You don't think so?"

"It can't happen. You want this and you know it's going to change your life. You can't be anything except either calm or excited, but definitely not scared. Scared of change? Yeah, well, I know they say we all are at some level, but I don't buy into to that, not when you know you are about to go into on/off mode. And I know you ain't scared of me doing the procedure!"

"Oh, no, not at all. Why wouldn't I trust you to cut into my brain and implant a foreign device that has never been tested before on anyone but you? Sure, I'm so good with your hairstyling skills that I move right into trusting you to perform neurosurgery on me. No worries at all."

"You are free to change your mind, but you know you can't. You are so hungry for this thing, you jonesing for it!"

"But what if I decided I don't like it? Can you take it out?"

"Good question. Probably not."

"What?"

"Well, it's a pretty delicate procedure and we don't want to be digging around in your brain more than once. If you don't want it, it's best to just turn it off remotely, but not go back in to remove it."

"Right. Okay, how does this thing work again?"

"It's a wireless device. The sensors are in your brain and the controls are in your wrist. Here, see how small they are? And, no it won't set off a metal detector, so you're good there."

I'm staring at what looks like a dime and an AAA battery with two tiny buttons on the side. The dime goes in my head and the AAA battery in my wrist.

"And you're sure I can't cure my inability to pursue my dreams with a shot of gin?"

"You'd need a lot of shots of gin. Then you'd never get anything done because you'd be a drunk. A drunk with a dream. Do you want some more time to think about this?"

"No, but do you have any gin?"

"Girl, you know I do!"

"Okay, I'll need about three shots and then my brain is yours."

"Three shots coming up."

Monique heads upstairs. I walk over to look at the device again. I must be really desperate for change. Wonder why I didn't just pray? I should do that now: Lord, you know my heart and you know I hate my job. I've prayed before for a change and for me to move forward with my dream to be a writer. I am sorry it has come to this, but then again, maybe this is where you led me? If not, please God, let this still go well and not kill me or anything. Thank you, Lord. In Jesus' name, I pray. Amen.

"Here you go! I'd take a shot with you, but that might make you nervous."

"Might?"

Monique is holding out a serving tray with a shot glass and a bottle of gin.

"Bottoms up!"

I take the first shot, then the next, and finally the third. And then I pour one more and down it.

"Four is a nice even number."

"I can't disagree with you. Are you ready?"

"Ready."

Monique points to the makeshift surgical table. I walk over and climb on top. As I'm getting comfortable, she positions a floor lamp over my head.

"Okay, scoot towards me. I need your head to hang off the table so I can have the best angle."

"Question. I just thought about this. How are you going to numb me?"

"Oh, I have a local anesthetic that I got from a friend who's a vet."

"Do I even want to know how?"

"Let's just say, you give and you get. It was a fair trade. Anyway, it's enough to knock out a St. Bernard. You're good. Don't worry; I got this. Now hold still…I need to numb you…okay, while this is kicking in, I'm going to shave just a small part of your head."

I feel the razor on my skin. I'm at peace. I want this.

"Okay, I'll walk you through what I'm doing, if that's okay, or would you rather not know?"

"Sure, that's fine."

"Well, now I'm using a scalpel to cut into your head. Do you feel anything?"

"No, not a thing…well, yeah like tugging, but no pain."

"That's good. I'm now placing the device inside your brain."

"I'm guessing there's more to this, right?"

"Yeah, but I'm keeping it in laymen's terms for you. Otherwise me getting all technical might worry you."

"Yeah, it just might."

"Alright, it's in place and I'm stitching you up now. First part is done! Girl, you were quiet."

"I didn't think I was supposed to be having a conversation with you."

"No, but you just locked up. So, let's see. We can test this before I put the control in your wrist. Can you tell a difference?"

"I just felt my body jerk a little and I feel really giddy."

"You're such a white girl with your language. 'Giddy.' That's cute. So you felt it? The switch? Here, how about now?"

"I felt that jerk again. Is that always going to happen?"

"Yeah, but you'll get used to it."

"I didn't even think to ask about the side effects…I must be crazy."

"Crazy better! Now how do you feel?"

"Inquisitive, serious."

"Cool, 'cause you're in left-brain mode. How about now?"

"I hope I adjust to this jerking, but giddy, again. So that's it, these changes will make me go from Top Secret to Bambi?"

"That's it. You'll start to notice within a week that you've got more of a flow going with it, but yeah. Now let's get this in your wrist. I'll have to shoot you up again."

I lay down again and Monique injects the needle to numb me. Then, after a few minutes, she cuts open a small slit in my wrist.

"Dang, girl, aren't you going to look away?"

"No, stuff like this doesn't bother me."

"Cool."

Monique finishes and sews up my arm. I take a look at my arm and see the two small buttons underneath my skin.

"Now, this is going be a little tender for a few days. I'm going to give you some liquid anesthetic to rub on before you change the controls. Apply it about five minutes beforehand. But they are really sensitive, so a very light touch like this should work." She lightly glides her finger over the buttons and I feel the change.

"Since you plan to stay in left-brain all day at work, you won't have to touch it really but twice a day. It should heal up really quickly. Also, I'm giving you a spare. If it's too painful, just use this one, and don't use the one in your arm until it's healed. Also, if for any reason the one in your arm should get damaged, then you have a backup. And, I have one for you here as well. Here, let's put you back to right-brain for now."

"Sure, okay. How would it get damaged, though?"

"It really shouldn't, but say you get a wild hair to go rollerblading and you take a bad fall and land on your wrist, well, then you should come see me to have it checked out."

"Okay…but, wait. It just occurred to me—one day, you might die before me! Then what? And why am I thinking about this in right-brain mode?"

"Because it doesn't turn off your brain, silly! You can still think, but if you'd notice, you're asking me this question and smiling at me. If you were in left-brain mode right now, you'd be freaking out."

"Ah, yes, I don't really seem to give a shit about it, but it seemed like something I should ask. I love this thing! On to my weave, right?"

"Yeah, I see you got that rich bitch hair again. You know you can pay half as much for the same look."

"The last time I bought cheap hair, it knotted up so bad. You remember that, right?"

"You just got a bad batch. It happens, but it shouldn't scare you into never buying it again. Anyway, let's get started. Thanks for washing your hair. That saves some time."

"Yeah, no worries. I need to be at work pretty early tomorrow, so whatever I can do to help move things along."

I'm now sitting in a pretty beat-down-looking salon chair while Monique begins braiding my hair, and says, "You know, I was shocked you wanted to do this during the week. I would have figured you'd want to wait until the weekend."

"No, I'm someone who needs to move forward without much time to contemplate things. If I do, it will take forever for me to make a decision."

"I hear ya. With this device, which by the way we need to give some cool-ass name, you will know what to do when you have some kind of decision to make, be it left- or right-brain mode. You'll be so in the zone in that mode, all things will come much easier for you."

"LR-7."

"What now?"

"The name for this thing. "L" for Left Brain and "R" for Right Brain and seven for the number of sex partners I've had. But it's your device. It should have a special meaning for you."

"Naw, that works 'cause it will help remind me that I am not as bad off as you!"

"What!"

"Girl, seven, really? Even my nerdy engineering ass was getting some on the regular. You'd better stay in right-brain for as long as you can everyday so you can up that number!"

"Up it how? You act like there are men out there just waiting for me to sleep with them?"

"Hello? There are."

"Well, I can't seem to meet any."

"Keep the LR-7 on right-brain mode and I promise you they'll be coming out the woodwork for your ass!"

Maybe Monique is right and I will loosen up with this device. It can't be any worse for me, though.

"Love it, as always. So, I guess we're done?"

"Done."

"How much for the hair?"

"It's on me. It's part of the procedure."

"Well, then I should have had you pay for my hair!"

"Only if you wanted the cheaper stuff! Now, for your outpatient instructions—go home and go to bed. You can stay in right-brain, but don't forget to switch to left before work in the morning. Keep your arm out of water and you can remove the bandage in the morning. The stitches will dissolve on their own in another week or so."

"Okay. I'll have to just tell Dan something."

"To fuck off?"

"One day, but I'll just tell him I burnt myself when I was cooking."

"Um-hum."

We head upstairs to the front door.

"Alright, let me get out of here. Thanks for the hookup."

"Alright, call me tomorrow and let me know how things are going."

"Okay."

I think I should have some high level of concern that there is a device implanted my brain with a control in my arm that Monique says is never coming out. That should make for an interesting autopsy someday.

As I enter the house my two lil' bits greet me with so much love.

"Hey, lil' ladies! Whatcha been up to while I was gone?"

As I let them out in the backyard I can feel my arm throbbing. I'm still good though, not an ounce of worry. I must be really fucked up mentally to be this nonchalant about everything that's just occurred in the last few hours.

15

LR-7 – Day One

~

The alarm is going off and I hit snooze a few more times before finally getting up and taking the dogs to the backyard. As I wait for them to do their business, I remove the bandage from my arm and rub my fingers over the two bumps. Bottom is left, top is right. Gotta remember that.

"Okay, let's go have breakfast!"

I take care of the dogs and then head back to the bedroom smiling and singing. I am so excited about my first day with LR-7. I get dressed, turn on the television for the girls, and head to the door.

"See you later! Home on time! Love you!"

I head up the street just in time as I see the bus rolling down the hill. I make it to the bus stop just as he pulls over. I walk up the steps and tap my Metro card, give the driver a sweet good morning smile, and walk a few seats back and take a seat. The ride to the Metro station is about ten minutes, just long enough for me to overhear the same conversation every morning between a woman and her two children: "Did you put your books back in your book bag? Where is the lunch I made for you? Please don't push your sister off the seat." Same dialogue, different day.

As I exit the bus at the Metro station, I take a newspaper from the nice man who is handing out the Washington Post's *Express*. It's my way of staying current. I'm not much for watching the nightly news, and these short articles are enough to keep me up to speed on the happenings in the world. I owe that to Dan. Before him, I really was adrift on what in the hell was happening. I like that he motivates me to be more, do more, and educate myself more, but I do hate that he's an ass.

I'm running my finger along the remote as I head up the escalator to the platform, but I can't bring myself to switch over. Maybe after I get off at the Pentagon. I need to ride this right-brain wave as long as I can.

The train arrives as soon as I make it to the platform and I enter and take a seat. I open the paper and scan each page, but then flip back to the last page, which contains the celebrity news and horoscopes. I begin reading and smiling to myself. Right-brain kicks ass! Who needs to start off the day reading about the horrors of the world or this country's failing or booming economy, depending on which way the wind turns.

The train is coming to a stop at the Pentagon. I reach over to my wrist and make the switch. There's a little tenderness but no pain. Man, Monique is good! My body jerks; I don't think it was noticeable to anyone, but it shouldn't matter since I don't know these people and I won't switch back until after work. I exit the train and head up the escalators. I am certain these Pentagon police officers won't check my badge. They are too busy chatting with each other and flirting with all the women. I feel safe here because I know God's got my back, but these guys have also taken out some folks, including a guy trying to enter the building with a gun. The freaky part of that was that I had just exited past the officers who took him out, not even five minutes prior, which is why I know God has my back.

I badge into the building and head upstairs to my office. So far, so good. I am feeling a bit more alert and am running through the list of things I need to get done today, something I don't typically do; normally, when I begin to think of the list before arriving at my desk, I shut it down. I like to delay getting into the bowels of this place until necessary. I guess that means this thing is still working.

I badge into the office and make my way to my desk.

"Hey, Al."

"Hey, Ava, what's up?"

"Not much. But I've got a lot to get done today. I have to set up for our All Call in a little bit, then I have a meeting with the Joint Staff folks, and then a meeting with my Army guy to discuss who pays for what for some overseas construction projects."

"That should make the day go by fast."

"I guess it should. What are you up to?"

"Hoping to finally brief our plan to Major General Deeds."

"Good luck. I need coffee."

I head back out of the office and over to the convenience store. I purchase my coffee and walk back to the office. I swing by my desk, grab my notebook and a binder, and head out again. I'm heading to the auditorium and, as I walk, I am calculating my day and laying out my strategy for this All Call as well and making notes about my next two meetings. I can't say I haven't done this in the past, but today I am super sharp about it, almost like I'm electronically cataloging these strategies in my brain; before the LR-7, I'd have random thoughts about what I needed to get done, coupled with a level of frustration that I was anticipating from having to go to these meetings.

As I enter the auditorium, I see Lt Col Brown and two tech sergeants.

"Looks like we've got everything in place and ready to go," I say to them. "Briefing, awards, award winners? Thanks, everyone, looks great."

"Yeah, the slides are up, the flags are in place, and the awards are laid out, so we're good," says Lt Col Brown. "Are you alright?"

"Sure, why do you ask?"

"'Cause you're, like, in robot mode today. Where's that smile and those silly jokes? You always make light of this stuff. It really keeps the tech sergeants from freaking out."

"Oh, yeah, I guess I just have a lot on my mind today. I've got a couple more meetings right after this, and I'm just not all here."

"Yeah, I hear you. Okay, looks like people are making their way in."

"I'll go check on Lieutenant General Green."

As I walk out of the auditorium I see Col Baker.

"Well, Ava," he says, "since you couldn't turn this thing off, I'm glad you were able to pull this together so quickly."

"Sure, sir. Sir, while we are waiting on Lieutenant General Green, I wanted to run some things by you. You know I have a meeting with my Army rep today and we will hammer out the details of the proposed MILCON (Military Construction) project."

"Yes. Tell me again—what project is this?"

Really wish I could switch modes right now...

"Here comes the General. I'll explain later, sir."

"Sure thing. Hello, sir!"

"Sledge, Ava. Are we ready to go?"

Col Baker slides in front of me.

"Yes, sir! My team has pulled everything together."

"Right, Sledge. Ava, thanks for getting this done. I know we normally give these duties to our military guys, but you can run circles around them."

"No problem, sir. We have your notes on the podium, and Lieutenant Colonel Brown will read off the award winners."

"Great, let's get moving."

Col Baker and I step aside, and let Lt Gen Green make his way inside. Once at the door, his exec announces his entrance.

"Attention! Lieutenant General Green."

The room comes to attention as Lt Gen Green walks to the front. Col Baker and I take a seat at the back of the room.

"Good morning, everyone."

As Lt Gen Green begins to speak and give out awards, I begin taking notes. They read: fair and equitable cost distribution, country memorandum of agreement, long-term maintenance of facility, future budget submissions, updated cost projection, go to credit union to open money market account, pick up glasses from optometrist.

I take a break from note taking as I hear Lt Gen Green wrapping up the awards.

"...and congratulations to all of our winners. Now that we are caught up, let's try to get next quarter's winners acknowledged on time. And speaking of on time, I am working on a new project. It is designed to show us how we fail to get stuff right. I have a few slides here that will help you see my point."

As Lt Gen Green goes through his briefing, I resume writing: stronger voice for the Services regarding theater plans, input for country priorities needed, Air Force capabilities not reflected well in current draft plan...

"Are there any questions?"

A major raises her hand and stands.

"Sir, if this is supposed to raise morale, don't you think this approach is a bit skewed? No offense, sir, but people are not normally driven to do better by being told they suck."

"That's an excellent question! I commend you for your insight; however, I must say since I've been at this for quite some time, this is indeed the best approach. As you progress in your career, you'll begin to see this as well, but excellent question. Anyone else? Come on now. This is the time. We're all the same in here, ask me anything, and don't be afraid that I outrank you. Be like the major here and ask away!"

A civilian raises his hand and stands.

"Sir, what are your feelings on the latest employee reductions?"

"Ah! Good question. Are you thinking tracking performance may lead to determinations on who is part of the reduction-in-force effort?

Because that's not the case at all! There are so many rules in place for how to fire a civilian and this is not one of them. It's all about tenure, really. Even if you are a lazy son of a bitch and you've been here forever, you're pretty much safe in knowing you'll keep your job…although, I do think OPM (Office of Personnel Management) is working to change this first-in-last-out rule and adopt something that looks at performance, but who knows when that will happen. Any more questions? No? Well, thanks, everyone!"

Lt Gen Green heads out and everyone rises to attention.

"Carry on."

I walk to the front of the auditorium to thank everyone for their help. As I head to the front, I quickly switch to right-brain mode. My body jerks, but I'm walking fast. I don't think it's noticeable.

"Thanks guys! You rock! Same time, next quarter? Don't forget, we love you, but you suck! Just kidding. But not really. Got to love this place, right? Hey, Steve, I'm feeling so groovy, I might just dance my way up to my next meeting!"

"Well, get your grove on then! But it's ten 'til, so you may just want to sprint."

"Shit! Okay, see you guys later. Thanks again! Treat yourselves to ice cream at lunch!"

I rush out and head down the hall and up a stairwell. I do my run-walk across the courtyard and up an escalator. I race down a corridor and open a conference room door. As I take a seat at the table, I lower my wrist under the table and switch to left-brain mode. My body makes a noticeable jerking movement, but I try to play it off with a loud cough.

Col Glen Davis runs these meetings. He's an Army guy who looks to be in his late sixties. I'm pretty sure that's not possible, even if he were prior enlisted turned officer, but he just looks old and tired. He's got the palest skin, full of deep wrinkles, and his once-red hair is nearly all white.

"Okay, folks. Let's get down to business. We had some serious issues resulting from our last war game. Our logistics were off and our fighter power was in the tank. I'm looking to the Air Force and Navy to clue me in here."

I speak first. "I think the issue is, sir, we play this joint war game but we don't actually play 'joint.' You know what I mean? Nothing was coordinated and we were in each other's cross hairs. We can't just call it 'joint,' we have to engage like 'joint,' like the Purple we are supposed to be."

The jackass Navy Captain chimes in after me. "True, we are not playing a joint game here at all, but I think the issue is, the Air Force couldn't prove their existence."

"Explain."

"You guys just want to assume you are going to fly in and hit some targets. We are far more strategic."

"If by 'strategic' you mean 'closer to the target by default than you are executing from a carrier,' then sure, but this game proved that not only do we need both sets of fighter power, but we also need to coordinate who hits what. Logic would dictate that you should have focused on the targets closest to your carrier and let us combat the outermost regions of the country. You can't just say, 'we have planes and we are going to fly them anywhere.'"

"I think we *can* say that and that is what we do."

"I think that is some bullshit and you know that is not part of any campaign strategy. As a matter of fact, if you'd referred to Annex C of the plan, you wouldn't have shitted this game up so badly. I propose we redo the air power portion of the game. Actually, we should re-look at everything from Phase 1 to Phase 5, to include logistics and comm, which didn't fare well in this game, either."

Col Davis is smiling and glaring at me, I'm guessing because no one ever uses curse words in the OSD/JS meetings—at least, none of the ones I attend. We are happy Purple Stepford People.

"Good points, Ava, but when do we have time to re-run the game?"

"I think the question is, why *don't* we have time to re-run the game? I mean, really, what the hell else are we doing? Rushing to get a report out based on a deadline we set that will serve no purpose because the game was a piece of shit? Perhaps if we actually got something right or close to right or at least acted like we gave a shit, then we'd have something worth reporting."

"Someone's on a roll today, but I just don't think leadership will approve of a redo. The cost alone."

"The cost? Really? We waste more money on everyone's monthly Blackberry bills."

"I don't want to play again. I think we should just write up the report," whines the Navy captain.

"Of course, you do. Look, I've got another meeting to get to. I don't have time for this. Either you redo this game or you'll get a non-concur from us on the report."

I stand up and leave the room. I can feel myself smiling. I love this device! Before this thing, I would have said something similar, but not with this straightforward hardassness; while there's limited cussing in meetings around here, we let it rip in our offices. Plus, you pushed back on a two O-6s, which are a rank higher than you. And threating to non-concur for the entire Air Force, shit, that's just nice! Ava, you kicked ass girl!

I walk down the hall and head down the escalator almost skipping. My next meeting is with Jeff and, judging by this last meeting, I'm sure we will nip this issue in the bud as well. I pick up the phone outside his office door to call him.

"Hi, Jeff, it's Ava. I'm outside your door. Thanks."

I wait a few seconds and Jeff appears. Jeff makes me sad. He, like Colonel Davis, is very pale in color and about sixty years old. He is also extremely overweight. He's always smiling, but he looks miserable; he's always out of breath, and his clothes are ill-fitting. He says he used to be larger than this, which only makes me feel worse for him.

"Ms. Ava, what's up?"

"Not much. Just left a Joint Staff meeting."

"How was it?"

"You mean, how wasn't it."

"Yeah, right."

"About this MILCON money. My leadership is not budging on what they feel they're responsible to pay. You know you guys will use the facility far more than we will, so what's with the big push to not fund more?"

"Because we can conduct our training about one hundred miles north and not build this facility, and don't really need it. We didn't plan for this, and will have to ask for special consideration to reallocate funding from another project to this one, thus delaying our effort on a project we really feel is necessary to our mission. And, we're Army. We can sleep outside in a tent. We're not prissy like you Air Force bubbas."

"Ha! I hear you, but we can't bankroll this whole thing, and you know as soon as we funded it 100 percent, you'd be back with your special requirements to make it work for you."

"True. We'll slap you with a big cost estimate. By the way, why do you guys have five different cost estimates?" I give Jeff a sheepish smile. "Anyway, I'm here to give you my leadership's 'no,' so I guess we can schedule a meeting with Policy and let them play mediator."

"Great, I've gone almost a month without having to deal with Marcy."

"Yeah, I noticed you've been AWOL from our meetings. Who's that guy that's coming in your place?"

"Oh, that's the new Colonel Select. He thinks he's the shit, so I figure, let him have at it."

"I wish I could pass my stuff on to someone else. Well, I'll let you go. I'll send Marcy an email and cc you this afternoon."

"Okay, let me walk you out."

"Thanks."

I leave and head down the hall. I turn to head to my office, but it hits me to make one more stop. I double back down the hall and, since I'm right at my front office—a term we use to designate where our 2- or 3-star generals reside—I might as well see if my office has any mail.

I've passed at least ten people on their cellphones heading to the front office. I am often impressed with the number of people who stand so intimately close to the windows when they attempt to use their phones. I guess whatever business they have going on must be really important for them to go through such an effort. I wouldn't want anyone to see me curled up on my phone in the hallway, but that's me. Plus, there's the courtyard, which, until it's the dead of winter and too cold to bear, makes more logical sense to me as a place to get good reception, but I don't know. There is the fact that Reagan airport is our neighbor, and it can be hard to hear when there are planes taking off every few minutes, but at least you're not looking like you're trying to French kiss one of the windows on the A Ring. I do wonder what people discuss in the middle of the day—doctor's appointments, lawyer, kids? Is it personal? Are they having deep conversations with their husband, wife, lover? My life is so tragically boring that I don't have anyone I need to speak to during the day. Sure there is the occasional gynecologist visit or mammogram that needs to be scheduled, but, depending on my mood, I have no embarrassment about making those calls from my desk, although I do try to wait until most are out of earshot.

I once had a boss ask me why I extended my leave request for a doctor's appointment. He asked in a way that implied I was somehow going to take the afternoon off and frolic around town. So, I told him that I was informed that the mammogram process now takes longer because they look at your images on the spot and determine whether further testing is necessary, meaning they have a much more thorough process of breast examination. He turned beat red and tried to shush me as I continued to lay out the process the hospital had explained. I, of course, being in a great pisstation spirit that day, just keep talking. Finally, when he refused to look me in the face anymore, I informed him I was heading for coffee.

I truly hate being here. I should have saved more when I was younger, learned the stock market. I should be a millionaire by now, but nope, I'm enslaved to the DoD. Well paid, but still enslaved.

I ring the bell for the office door and hear the click signaling the door is open. I walk in and see Steve at the copier.

"Hey, Steve, I thought since I was just down the hall, I'd stop and see if our office had any mail."

"Yeah, there's some stuff for you guys."

I'm flipping through a magazine as Maj Gen Deeds walks out of his office.

"Ava! Great job this morning. I'm glad Lieutenant General Green got his project launched, though I was really hoping you'd kill it. Are you losing your touch?"

"Probably, sir. Sir, I just met with the Army and they are not budging on the funding for the MILCON project. I'm going to set up a meeting with you and their general to discuss prior to taking this to Policy."

"Sounds good. Just write me up some talking points and I'll be good to go."

"Of course, sir. I'll have it to you later today."

"Thanks, Ava. Steve, I'm heading to the gym."

"Yes, sir."

As Maj Gen Deeds leaves the office I can hear him greeting someone in the hallway. I grab my notebook and the mail and realize I hadn't spoken to the administrative assistant. I look, and see Steve with his back towards me, so I do a quick switch to right-brain mode. I should ask Monique whether it is okay to switch this often. I am pretty sure she thought I'd stay in left-brain all day at work.

"Hi, Amanda. How are you today?"

"Good, how are you?"

"Good and busy, but no complaints. How's your daughter doing?"

"Oh, she's great! Just got engaged! We are all incredibly happy for her. I've already started planning the wedding and it just happened two days ago."

"That's great! Congratulations! You'll have to keep me posted on everything. I always wanted canary yellow for my wedding color."

"I certainly will, and tell me you are kidding? Seriously? Canary yellow?

"Yep, with the dresses in a 1950s look. Think of the movie, *When Peggy Sue Got Married*, all in canary yellow!"

"Ava, you're crazy."

"It can work. Think about it! See you guys later."

I walk out of the office and head down the corridor rubbing my wrist, mumbling to myself...Maybe this is a mistake. I'm too focused. I couldn't even relax to say hi to Amanda without switching...Maybe Monique should have made a middle of the road button. I can't keep switching back and forth just to have short chitchat...Plus, my wrist is still sore, as this just happened last night...

MY DAY ENDS with a therapy session. I am waiting in the lobby for Dr. Smith and staring at a text I just sent to Monique, asking if I should use left or right for therapy. ("Right, right?") I am desperate for a reply, but I get nothing before I hear Dr. Smith approaching the door, so I toss the phone in my purse. I switched to right-brain mode right after work, and I'm banking on it being the correct mode for therapy, but I don't fucking know. Maybe therapy should be in left-brain mode. Maybe I just need to be more matter of fact, more logical with my shitload of problems. Oh well, even if I guessed wrong, how much damage could one session do? Hell, I'm sure I'll be in therapy for quite some time.

"Ava, hello. Come in."

"Hi, Dr. Smith. How are you?"

"Good, and you?"

"I'm existing."

"That's not very encouraging."

"I'm feeling less than encouraged."

"Well, have a seat and let's talk."

I move to sit in an overstuffed armchair as Dr. Smith positions herself across from me in a simple wooden chair.

"So, tell me about your existence."

"You know that when I first started therapy, it was because I couldn't get over this jerk of a guy I was hung up on. Now, here we sit a few years later, and I have more problems than I did when I first started seeing you. I don't think I'm a good therapy patient."

"Why would you say that?"

"I know you think if I just keep on talking, I'm going to come to the answer, but it seems like every time, I do, and then what? I repeat the crazy and we start over again. I think I'm hopeless. I am determined to have a crappy life."

"You don't actually believe this shit do you? Name five good things about your life. Come on, give me that much tonight."

"I'm alive, I have the world's best dogs, I have a good job, and well, that's about all I can give you."

"That's a nice start. Let's go with those for now. I know you're happy to be alive and I know you love your dogs, so let's talk about your job. Most people would be proud to say they work at the Pentagon, that they support our nation's defense. Does that give you any sense of accomplishment?"

"Not even close. I love that I'm a part of our nation's defense—I just don't feel that what we do there has any real bearing on that, you know?"

"No, I don't. Please explain."

"We are the headquarters for the Defense Department, but the real work is done by those who are deploying, and in the field, and out to sea. We answer a bunch of questions from the Hill and formulate budgets that are never approved, and every time we act as if the questions are brand new, and we run around like crazy people trying to coordinate an answer that, nine times out of ten, is the same answer we gave before, and we have the nerve to be surprised when our budgets are disapproved. It's like I'm stuck in the Pentagon version of the movie, *Groundhog Day*."

"Ava, for the last few years we have talked about your love life, and it's interesting that tonight you are opening up about your work life. You know, when I've asked you before, you've always said work was fine, and if your personal life was half as good as your work life, you'd be a happy camper. This is good that you are now feeling comfortable to open up about this."

"Sure, but I am not sure I need to add to my list of problems. Besides, people would think I am just crazy anyway. I've got me one of them good ol' government jobs with good benefits—what do I have to complain about? For me, I'm just there, in Shawshank. Maybe, though, it's time to move on. I don't know. But, really, what's there to complain about?"

"Sounds like plenty. You started off by saying that you have more problems than when we began. There's your love life, your job, and is there something else?"

"A whole lot more, but it doesn't matter."

"Why would you say that? And why are your referring to the Pentagon as 'Shawshank'?"

"Because I've been coming here long enough to know it's all interrelated, right? That the core of it all is all the same. Shawshank. Like the movie *The Shawshank Redemption*. It's like prison. We even have a courtyard where we can roam around outside and look up at the sky."

"That's usually the case, yes. The core of your issues is usually the same, but if there is something more, it's okay to talk about that too—if you feel comfortable, that is. And then we can visit your prison reference."

"Shawshank. Because we are prisoners of the bureaucracy, only we earn nice salaries, but most of us are completely dependent on our paychecks, so we're enslaved. Can't leave because we have to make money, and can't get another job because all we know is the DoD. As for my other problems, maybe another night."

"Okay, if that's what you want."

"I want something. I don't know what exactly, but I am tired of not having it. I am tired of coming here week after week, month after month, year after year discovering my issues and then screwing it up again. I am tired of saying I want a good man in my life, but I wait anxiously for the jerk I'm dating to give a damn and want to spend time with me. I want to do that thing where I'm so freakin' in love with myself that I radiate love all the damn time and I can't help but attract a good-ass man into my life. That's what I want."

"This is possible, Ava. You just have to keep working to get there."

"But I keep backsliding and I am tired of myself. I just want to move forward and keep on going that way. And I want a new job. Andy escaped and Red was finally paroled. If I don't do something soon, I'm going to die in that place. Or when I finally do get out, I'll feel so out of touch, like Brooks, that I'll commit professional suicide and find myself at the unemployment office."

"You've been at the Pentagon for a while now, yes?"

"Eight years. I should have sat for the CPA exam. Then I would be off doing something far better than working in the five-sided bureaucratic prison, or rather, plantation. They call it the Reservation, but to me, 'plantation' is more accurate.

"It's never too late to change careers."

"I don't want to be a CPA. I just want to be in love. If I were in a happy, loving relationship, then my job could suck, but I'd have him, and he'd be enough."

"I think you know that would more than likely not be the case."

"I'd like to think so, anyway. For now, I get Dan, who may or may not take an interest in me for sex."

"Do you believe Dan is the best you can have?"

"I believe Dan is the best I am willing to let myself have."

"And, why is that?"

"Self-esteem issues."

"Ava, give me some credit here after all these years. Is that all you have to say?"

"I know we've discussed more, but really, I can't move past the fact that I don't think much of myself. I try. I have all these affirmations, but at the end of the day I don't believe them and I don't love myself very much and I don't see how I can ever be that woman who has that great life. I can fantasize about it, but it just doesn't stick in my subconscious."

"Do you think that's why you are still at a job you are not fond of?"

"I want to believe I can do other things, but I'm just a well-paid government employee. I have an accounting degree, but didn't take the CPA exam. I have an MBA, but didn't bother to get a concentration."

"Can you recall why? Why no CPA exam or concentration?"

I look at my watch and rise from the chair.

"Yes, but I see my time is up. I'd better go."

"Ah, yes, but we will pick up right here next time."

DAN IS MAKING steak and I'm sitting on a bar stool drinking wine. We sure do have a fucked-up relationship.

"I'm beginning to think you only see me because I'm down the street from your therapist."

"That does have a lot to do with it. I know we are just a few miles apart, but it's just easier when I'm already a few stops away."

"You should just move here and get out of Virginia. I don't know why you think you need to live in a big house like that."

"Because."

"Because of the dogs, I know, but that just doesn't make sense. They're not big dogs that need a lot of space. I think you are just using that as an excuse. You know, there are some units for sale in this building."

"Ha! Why in the world would I want to live in the same building as you? Don't you think that would be awkward when you decide to go into one of your 'I'm not speaking to you' modes?"

"I call it my 'adult time-out.'"

"Whatever."

"So, how was your day?"

"Crazy. The senator is on some rant about these lobbyists. They are all about clean fossil fuel, which he was all about until he got a notion to run for president, and now he's siding with the crazies who believe we can just abuse the planet and die and to hell with future generations. Talk about flip-flopping."

"That's the way of the world for most, I guess. But I can't imagine he thinks he's going to get far without having some eco-friendly softer side."

"Yeah, well, he does and all I can say is, I'm glad I won't be a part of it much longer."

"Really? Why not?"

"I've decided to go into real estate full-time. I used to dabble in it while I was in law school, and I think it's time to go back to it. I'd rather hustle at that than hustle for a nut in a suit."

"Wow! That's great! I wish I could do something like that."

"Why can't you?"

"I don't have anything else to do. Well, except writing, but that's not the same as having a real estate license."

"It is if you hustle the same. Don't sell yourself short like that. Dinner's ready. I've got your steak medium well."

"Ah! You are such an excellent cook!"

"I'm excellent at some other things, too."

Dan is unbuckling his pants. I really just want to eat dinner.

"Also, I know how you like your sausage, nice and hard and well done."

"True, but don't you want to eat first?"

"Yeah, I can eat some dessert first before dinner."

Dan is standing behind me unbuttoning my blouse with one hand and tugging at my panties under my skirt with the other. I let out a sigh and then turn to face Dan. I wrap my arms around his neck and make a move to switch to left-brain mode and my body jerks.

"See, I knew you wanted some of this before dinner. I felt that tremble just now."

Why left-brain mode for sex with Dan? Because there's no emotion involved anyway. We both have put up walls so high that there's no getting to our hearts. I might as well see what happens when I'm in work mode. Left-brain is strong and runs shit like in my meetings today. I'm about to be the one to run some shit in this condo for a change.

I grab Dan by the hand and lead him to the bedroom. I unbutton his shirt and then yank his pants down.

"Oh, yeah, I knew you wanted this!"

Dan motions for me to go down on him, but instead I grab him by the shoulders and force him to his knees. I slide off my skirt, lower my panties and grab his face.

"Tonight, it's all about me. I want you to stay down here until the neighbors hear me screaming your name."

"Damn, Ava. Okay, we can switch shit up, but you'll owe me. You know I always gets mine first."

"Not tonight, sweetie, and not if you ever want this again. Now, shut the fuck up and do me."

Dan is on his knees giving me pretty good head, but I'm not satisfied. I move to the edge of the bed and instruct him to work harder as I lean back.

"You can do better than that. Don't just lick me, suck me stick your tongue deep inside me. Make me want to fuck you."

He's doing better, hell, he's about to make me scream his name, so I pull his head back, and motion for him to join me on the bed.

"Fuck me hard and deep and don't stop until I tell you to."

The look in his eyes is both rage and ecstasy. Dan is all about control in every part of his life and I know this is killing him, but it's also making him horny as hell.

I keep instructing him, which position, how hard, how fast, stop and give me more head. Our bodies are dripping in sweat, and our moans are so loud I'm sure the people passing by on the street can hear us. He screams my name, "Ava, damn, shit!"

"I need a little more."

"What?"

"You need to give me some more head, now."

"Yes, ma'am."

As I lie there with my legs spread wide and Dan delighting me, I feel all the sensations, but not one once of emotion. This is good, there's no "why won't he love me, propose to me, give a shit about me." It's just some damn good sex. You couldn't have told me that's all this would end up being, a sexual, dysfunctional relationship, when we met. I still recall that time so vividly.

There's a restaurant in the basement of the building that some know about and many do not. It's become special to me mainly because most don't know about it. It's nice and quiet and fast to order and get out, or sit and enjoy your meal. This wonderful place went through a renovation in the summer of 2010, and I had to look elsewhere for my morning coffee and breakfast. Being a little lazy, I didn't venture far, just upstairs to the Sbarro on the third floor. I walked in, and immediately I saw him. I had seen him around the building before and thought to myself, what an incredibly fine man, but we never made eye contact, and it was clear that I was not someone that caught his attention. I relished the pleasure of seeing some nice eye candy in the building and moved on.

But this day, he was there sitting with a group of guys, all of them in their flight suits and all looking as egotistical as you can imagine a group of pilots looking. I quickly walked past without looking his way and made my way up to the counter to order. Oh look, they now make a spinach and feta breakfast wrap. Sounded good, so I ordered it along with my vanilla latte. As I waited for my order I did everything but look his way, which, in the Sbarro's, is not much to do. After exhausting myself with looking aimlessly at the chef preparing the orders, I finally turned in his direction.

Since his back was to me, I could just shamelessly stare for a moment. Once my order was ready, I headed back out, but now I was nervous about my walk. I was strutting around in my four-inch Jessica Simpson heels, and for the first time in all my years in this building, I was nervous about a potential trip and fall. But hell, I had to leave, and I just started walking. As I passed his table, I couldn't help but glance his way. He looked up as I passed, probably because my heels were calling attention to me with the click and clack they were making. He didn't smile, but gave that black folks' head nod of acknowledgement. I did the same with a faint smile and swung my hips extra hard as I walked down the stairs and out the door.

A few days later, I passed him as I was heading for coffee at the convenience store down the hall from my office, and he spoke: "Hello." I replied with a "Hi." He said, "Take it easy," as he was heading towards the Metro entrance of the building. As he walked by, I nearly tripped. What the hell? Really, Ava? Are you that caught up with some fine-looking, seemingly arrogant pilot?

Yep, I was.

Fast-forward to a week later and I'm walking through the courtyard taking a well-deserved break and my badge holder falls apart. Everything hits the ground, badge, CVS card, credit card—I keep way to much stuff in it and use it like a wallet.

As I kneel down and start picking everything up, I hear a voice.

"Do you need any help?"

As I look up into the hot August sun I see him. It is as if he were bursting with rays of light. I couldn't see his face for the brightness of the sun and the shadow his body was casting around it, but I knew it was him. He bent over and gathered a few of my things and handed them to me. I said thank you, and then noticed his posse of pilots were standing just a few feet behind him. He asked if he could walk with me, and I said yes. As we parted ways from his co-workers, we walked toward the 4th corridor.

I don't recall a word we said in the courtyard, but once we were inside the building he introduced himself.

"My name is Dan, and I'm a pilot."

Normally my thought would have been, 'No shit, you're in in a flight suit,' but no sarcastic thoughts entered my mind. Plus, in all fairness, navigators and space guys wear flight suits, too. Maybe he wasn't being arrogant—maybe.

I gave him my name and my number, and he said he would give me a call that night. Looking back, though, just the fact that he had to point out the fact that he was a pilot was a clue of arrogance, or insecurity, or insecurity resulting in arrogance, but that's how it is around this place. In any case, I wouldn't be clued in to Dan's deeper issues until much later. I would also learn that he is a reservist who was in the building doing his reserve duty, and that his day job chief of staff for a senator.

And tonight he's my lover, nothing more. Funny, there was a time when I thought he'd be my everything.

16

Doctor Smith's Office, Again

~

"What's with the big smile on your face?" asks Dr. Smith.

"I left here the other week with this big breakthrough, but there was more, and today it hit me. I have the same dysfunctional relationship with my job as I do with men."

"Go on."

"I give and give and give. I work hard and work late nights and take work home and for what? For nothing to ever get better. That place is a magnified version of my entire existence! I give my body to Dan and my mind to the Pentagon and neither gives a damn about me. To be honest, I have a dysfunctional relationship with myself, too. That's why I've been stuck all this time. I didn't even major in something I cared about in college. I actually did what I knew would please my parents."

"You mentioned before that you didn't sit for the CPA exam or choose a concentration for your MBA."

"Right, because I had no desire to major in accounting or get an MBA. Because to date I have been living out the dreams of everyone but me. Amazing, considering my parents recently told me they never expected me to get this far. That all the success I had they thought would be part of my sister's life. They actually told me they never thought I would amount to anything! And the funny part is if I had known that, I would have gone after my dream a long time ago."

"Fuck, yes! You've nailed it! This is great! Tell me more."

"I seek some type of approval from everyone in my life. I can blame it on my parents who didn't love me enough, and the resulting low self-esteem, but the bottom line is I seek unattainable, emotionally unavailable men and things; well, with the exception of my two dogs and they're the only two things I didn't seek out. I was just minding my business and a lady at work walks up with Cleo, my poodle, and another time, I ran into a lady in the restroom at work and she said she remembered me saying I wanted a Yorkie, and then I had Sophie. When I am not trying to do anything, good things come, and when I am hungry for something, I get crap. Isn't that something?"

"It sure is. Why do you think that is?"

"Because I seek what is familiar, which is emotionally unavailable people, and then I work really hard to prove my worthiness to them. When I am just me, I attract good stuff. Do you know that I left a great job and a fabulous set of employees to take the job at the Pentagon?"

"No. I didn't realize that. Please tell me more."

"I had a great job, was a year away from a great promotion, and I left. I said it was to get away from a jerk of a boyfriend who got a woman pregnant while we were broken up for the hundredth time, but that wasn't it at all. I was doing great things and I was in charge of a lot of people and I had the ear of our general. My staff loved me and I was a damn good boss! When I left, they gave me the best going away anyone had ever had at that base; even the general came to say goodbye and presented my going away gift. I was finally feeling loved and accepted, and while it wasn't from my family or a man, it was from my work family, and I think that scared the hell out of me. I used the jerk of guy thing as an excuse. Didn't I?"

"Did you? Why are you questioning your decision?"

"Because he really hurt me and in the end, after he said he only wanted to be with me, he left one night and said he'd see me the next day, and I didn't hear from him again for months. He married her, the one who was pregnant. He left. He said he'd see me the next day and then he married her. He had just proposed to me and he left me. And, I had told my family about our engagement that night. I was hurt and embarrassed, so I just needed a new start right?"

"New starts can be a good thing."

"But I ran away. I mean, how many people get cheated on and or divorced, and they don't move to the other side of the country. But I told myself I needed this change, and there was nothing keeping me in Oklahoma, nothing."

"Nothing?"

"Nothing but a great network of friends, a great new house I had just purchased, and a great job that was leading me to a great promotion within a year. Yeah, nothing. You can't get rid of hurt and pain by changing your address; the bad choices come with you to your new residence. That's all I did, change locations and bring my mess halfway across the country."

"You know, it takes a brave person to pick up and move to a new city where she knows no one and to walk bravely into that huge building to start a new job. Don't sell yourself short for all you have accomplished since moving here."

"Sure. I keep seeing everywhere lately these quotes about how you can't grow if you're comfortable. Maybe I needed to leave Oklahoma, and the jerk guy was just the catalyst."

"Life has a way of making us move even if we don't think we're ready. And, remember, regardless of why you left, you are here now."

"Yes, and I don't want to be. I am very comfortable working at Shawshank, so if those quotes are right, then it's time to go. In either case, my sex life and my work life are sad, and I have no love life. Which is all I've ever wanted since I was a little girl. I want to change this."

"We can do that, but first I want to make sure you are clear on what it is you want to accomplish."

"I want to finally love myself. I want to know without a shadow of a doubt I am enough, that I bring a lot to the table, be it at work or in my personal life. I want to be open and honest and not be attracted to dysfunction. The men I want relationships with are dysfunctional and the bureaucratic Shawshankland is dysfunctional. I want to be so functional that I repel dysfunction. Iyanla Vanzant once said on Oprah, 'You attract what you put out,' and I am tired of putting out dysfunction."

"That is a very true statement."

"But how do I get there and why has it taken me all this time to figure this out? I told you, I am bad patient."

"You're not a bad patient. Everyone comes to this place at their own speed. I have patients who have been seeing me for decades and are still not there. Don't stress yourself with a timeline for change. Just find peace in knowing you got here, and from here, your world will be different."

"I desperately want that."

"Then let's get started, shall we?"

"Yes, let's."

My session with Dr. Smith was amazing, but I know I will fall back into my rut soon. I love, though, the way she gets so excited, as if it's the first time I've had this revelation.   Anyway. I'll try very hard to stick to it this time.

17

FREAKAZOID!

~

It's Friday, and I'm going to get my twerk on!

I've made it to another week's end and since there's no happy hour this week, I'm heading to FREAKAZOID!, which is an over-the-top, totally awesome, better-than-Zumba-could-ever-be dance exercise class. A year ago Sheryl invited some of us to join her here and, not thinking much about it, I showed up and was ready to partake in a good dance workout. To my surprise this class was a street dancing underground erotic zone of wildness. Not the best way to describe it, but it ain't no Zumba class, or as their T-shirts say, it ain't no week ass dancing. The intensity is high and the songs—all unknown to me, with the exception of one or two—have a rawness to them that make the class even more intriguing. We twerk, we shake, we roll, we glide, we grind, and mostly, we sweat. It's like going to the club, but with a much cheaper cover charge. Really, they turn the lights off and have a few club lights going, so it's amazing.

I'm shaping up well with this class, but I'm still am not happy with my weight. I'm up to 125 and while my clothes say size 2 or 4, I feel fat and unattractive. I turn heads every day and yet I feel like shit. I think it is because of Dan. As a matter of fact, I know it is. He doesn't say I'm fat; he just says I can do some cardio to get rid of this water weight I have. Of course he's put on some weight since we met, but he believes he's perfect.

Dan makes me feel fat (Dr. Smith would correct me and say I allow myself to feel this way). And while the sex is great, he's a one-trick pony—well, except for the other night when I worked him out in left-brain mode. Yet, I internalize my extra few pounds as a reason why he might lose interest in me. He claims he can only release himself if we do it doggy-style, but I think it's his way of avoiding intimacy, or at least that's what an article I read said. For five years we've only done it doggy-style, with the exception of a handful of times when he attempted another position. It really is quite pathetic. Pathetic, for both of us. How bad off am I if I am holding out hope for this man who cannot look me in the face when we have sex?

I do wonder how in the hell I can rationally think this shit and still allow him anywhere near me. I really do think therapy is working, but damn, it's taking a long time for me to shake his ass. And if I can think this, why in the hell can't I just shake his ass? Self-esteem was something I learned about in middle school, but learning what the hell it is and actually doing something to have a healthy self-esteem are two different things. Maybe this device will allow me to shake him once and for all.

18

Surprise

~

I've been stuck in this MILCON meeting for a week and I am certain it is pointless, but nonetheless, here I sit. I take comfort in the fact that everyone is giving Marcy hell this week. I shouldn't think this way, but she's intolerable. These university grads who arrive here as political appointees or some shit like that who don't know shit about the military and are running the show—can someone explain how this makes any sense? I am truly amazed how this all doesn't just collapse, but it's probably extremely hard to kill a bureaucracy. When this is over, I'm heading to my basement haven for a bacon cheeseburger and fries.

"Ava."

"Hey, Jeff."

"Hey, before this thing wraps up, can you chat with me about the MILCON project?"

"Sure."

I'm sitting with a handful of folks in a side room away from Marcy and the crazy crew. This allows me to see and hear the discussion via the monitors, but have a bunch of side bar conversations with others and make this week somewhat productive. Jeff's been in and out all week. I think his tolerance for this shit has completed dissolved.

"I see we are on to have our generals discuss this issue next week," says Jeff.

"Yeah, that was the soonest I could get them together."

"That's great actually. It gives me time to get my guy prepped. He has to know all the little details. That's why I've been a ghost most of this week."

"Oh, I thought you'd just had enough of all of this."

"I'd had enough of this before I switched uniforms, but it's been getting in to see him every time he has a few minutes that's kept me away from this year's Oscar-winning performance. Do I have to guess who won Best Actress? Probably the same gal from last year and the year before from that COCOM that...I'll just stop now before I say too much."

"Yep, Darlene wins again this year. This year, though, we got a lot of extra behind-the-scenes descriptions of why only their projects are worth funding. It could have been moving had she dug just a little bit deeper for some real tears!"

"This whole thing is really sad."

"Well, I'm glad I don't have your issue with my guy, though I'm not sure which is worse, being in here or sitting with my 2-star all week. But I must say my guy is easy. Give him a few notes and he's good to go regardless of if he actually has a clue as to what's really going on."

"I only wish that were my case."

"Thank you all for coming, and we will send out minutes early next week."

I hear Marcy wrapping up the meeting, and smile.

"Well, Jeff, there's a bacon cheeseburger calling my name."

"Let me get out of your way."

"See ya!"

I LOVE MY basement haven. There's never anyone from Shawshank down here, and I love joking with the haven's staff. I've tried doing this in left-brain mode, but it's just not working, so, back to the right for a few minutes. Oh, and I still need to check in with Monique about all this switching.

"Hey, what's up?" I say, waving and smiling at the cook as I enter. He and I go way back to my first year here.

"Hey, not much. What's it for today? Grilled cheese on white or bacon-cheese burger?"

"I really don't stray, do I?"

"Nope. You've been getting one of these two things for years now."

"Yeah, I guess I have. I am a creature of habit. Today is a celebration day, so you know what that means."

"Bacon cheeseburger and fries coming up!"

"Thank you!"

"What's the celebration?"

"Surviving a week-long extremely boring and unproductive meeting."

"Really, what was it about?"

"Military construction."

"Oh, now, that's important stuff, ain't it?"

"Only if you want it to be."

"You only want mustard and no veggies? And fries with a lot of seasoning salt?"

"Yep, same as usual."

"You really are a creature of habit."

"Yeah, I doubt I'll ever change."

"Never say 'never'!"

"Of course, you're right. Anything good could make me change my ways."

"That's right. And you got to be ready 'cause you never know when or what that might be."

"True, very true."

"Okay, but today one very plain bacon cheeseburger and way-too-salty fries."

"Thank you, sir!"

I pay for my lunch and grab some utensils and packs of ketchup from the counter.

"Can you please tell me why ya'll's ketchup only has a baby squirt in each pack? I have to take ten just to eat about five fries!"

"'Cause this is the government and we cheap like that!"

"True! See ya!"

As I'm heading up the escalator I move to switch back to left-brain mode. Damn all this switching.

"Hey, Ava!" Great, it's my least favorite zipper-suiter.

"Hey, Nerf Ball!"

Great, a fake smile and wave, and he keeps it moving, unlike most days.

"Zipper-suits" is the name given to pilots because of the flight suits they wear, which can also be a not-so-obvious way of saying "dumbasses," "arrogant bastards," or something to the liking. They know what we think of them and I have no idea what they really think about it, nor do I care.

What I do care about is why they think it's okay to strip down in the middle of the office, like it's an all men's squadron, to change in the morning and in the evenings. They seem disturbed that I don't look embarrassed or stay in my cubicle until they're done, but I don't have time for them. I'm not going to delay my comings and goings based on their need to wear civvies (civilian clothes) to and from work. Plus, they just stand there and talk, so who knows how long I'd be hanging out waiting for them to be "decent." It does piss me off a little that 99 percent of them are fine as hell. I wonder if that's some kind of unspoken criteria for being a pilot in the Air Force? And, more curious, the fighter pilots are hotter than the fine-ass bomber and tanker pilots. Interesting.

Again, I digress, but since I have, I also hate call signs, as I've said before, which is mainly a fighter pilot thing. If I don't know your name, I can't email you, and can't send you a meeting invite, but this is how a typical conversation with them goes:

"Hey, Flapjack needs to attend the next meeting we have with the general on subject none of this matters anyway. We just saw Poncho in the hall and he noted to add him and Grits to the list as well. Can you add them to the distro list?" *No, fuckhead, I can't because I don't know who in the hell you are talking about! I wasn't stationed with Flapjack five years ago and I didn't graduate from the Academy with Poncho and I didn't go to flight school with Grits. Give me some real-ass names, you dumb fucks! No, I am not part of your non-elite zipper-suit club and I don't want to be. I just want to do my damn job and go home to my dogs.*

Enslaved in foolishness.

Zipper-suits and call signs. I am not a fan of Air Force pilots—none of them. Some think the fighter pilots are the most arrogant, but they are all assholes to me. Fighter pilots love to say in meetings, "I'm just a dumb fighter pilot, but my thinking about this is...*Yes, you are, you don't need to tell us this because we know you're a pilot and just shut the hell up,* but they just keep talking. Dan is the same way; he's an F-15 guy.

Anyway, I'm back at my office and ready to have a few moments of silence with a burger and fries.

I've spent this week in the bowels of the building, literally on the mezzanine level. It's been a long and painful week of OSD, Joint Staff, the COCOMs and the Services hashing out the future requirements for military construction. To treat myself for enduring the week I am about to tear into this bacon cheeseburger and fries. It's Friday. I'm ready to end this week and I'm going to spend the next few hours in this building savoring this food and typing up my notes from the week. But, maybe not, since Maj Gen Deeds is now standing at my desk with a handful of the folks from the office.

"There she is."

"Hello, sir. We just wrapped up the MILCON meeting. It wasn't as painful as last year. I think it helped that we got together as an Air Force and discussed our issues beforehand."

Maybe if I give more info, the awkwardness of Maj Gen Deeds and these people might just go away. What in the hell are they all standing here for?

"Yep. That was genius of you to think to do that. That's what got you the Employee of the Quarter award."

Sadly, it did. I received an award for thinking we should have our shit together before taking on the rest of the DoD. What's sadder is, no one thought of it before me.

"So…I will type up my notes and send them to you later today."

"Yeah."

"Yeah."

"Ava," he finally blurts out, "you've been selected as a fellow for the FY15 Fellowship program. You will be at Big Brains Research, Inc. Aren't you excited?"

"Yeah, they have primaries and alternates for those."

"Yeah, and you are the primary."

"Oh."

I really want to tear into my burger and fries as the smell is overwhelmingly inviting.

"Oh. Okay."

"Aren't you more excited than that?"

"Sure. I think I am in shock."

"Why? You deserve this Ava."

Everyone is standing around smiling and amused at my lack of excitement. I want to get excited, but things like this just don't happen for me. It's hard to take this in. I really just want my food because I'm starving, but they won't leave, so I'd better fake the funk.

"Wow! Okay. I'm getting there. I'm excited. Gee, this is awesome!"

They still won't leave.

"Yes, it is. Well, congratulations. You're going to be spending a year in Southern California. That's freakin' awesome!"

"Yes, it is. Sorry, guys, I am just in too much shock to fully digest all of this."

Others now pipe in.

"Congrats, Ava!"

"Thanks."

"Yeah, congrats. I'm jealous."

"Oh, thank you."

They are now walking away, but Maj Gen Deeds is still standing at my desk.

"You're going places, Ava."

"Sure, sir."

"I mean it. You are going to kick butt out there and come back here running things, even more than you do now."

"Well, I'm just happy for the opportunity."

"Ok, enjoy that burger and fries. You got yourself a celebratory meal and didn't even know it."

"Yep, thanks, sir."

Thank goodness, they're gone! I'm starving. I wish I could get just a little bit more excited, but it ain't happening right now.

I'll email my friends and tell them. Surely that will get me pumped by seeing their reactions. Oh, and I'll have to tell Dan. We are in such a good place now; like a real dysfunctional couple. I hope this doesn't ruin that for us. But, I have to go. I'm not crazy to think I should turn this down for him and he's not made any move toward a real commitment. Maybe this will bring us to that point. Maybe he'll realize how much he loves me once the thought of me being gone for a year is rolling around in his head. Maybe.

With my pod area clear of my co-workers I open the container and inhale the wonderful aroma of bacon. I'm eating and typing this email to my friends at the same time. I'm feeling rather rushed because I need some form of validation from them. Something more than "congrats" and "you deserve this," but from the sister girls I'm going to get back things like "His plans are the best plans" and "God has so much more for you beyond this." I need those types of words right now, not the standard "you're on your way" bullshit. We all know people who were selected for these types of programs and years later they are still working at the same grade and even returned to the same job. I don't think anyone is just trying to get rid of me either as we all know those people too – those who get selected for programs or promotions to be gotten rid of. That's why I need my girls to weigh in.

The first one to hit me back is Marva: "God is shining on you so brightly! Amen!" Next is Terry: "You know He's got those steps in order, girl!" Then Dana: "Amen, praise God, another one of us is freed from this plantation!"

Alright, I'm good now. This is real and it's happening. I think I'll add to my celebratory burger and fries with a hot fudge sundae from McDonald's. Normally my hot fudge sundaes are reserved for super stressful days, but today is a good day to switch things up. But wait, Sprinkles, the cupcake shop, is in the building this week. Hum, yep, Sprinkles it is!

I'm wrapping up my lunch and reading more "hallelujah" and "praise God" email replies. It's Friday again and I'm definitely going to hit FREAKAZOID! as it also serves as a club night for me: $5.00 a class is cheaper than any cover charge, and I don't have to look cute to get my party on.

I'll give Dan a call when I get home. I'm sure he'll be excited for me.

19

The Call

~

"Ava-Flava, what's up!"

Years ago, Dan gave me this crazy hip-hop nickname after learning of my love for groups like 2 Live Crew and Naughty by Nature back in the day.

"Nothing, just wanted share some news with you. I've been selected for a fellowship with Big Brains, Inc. in California."

"What? That's great! Congrats!"

"Thanks."

"I told you you'd be going places."

Oddly, Dan's response is more generic and lifeless than Maj Gen Deeds's had been.

"Thanks. Anyway that's all. I've got some planning to do since I will have to report in July."

"July? Ava, it's November."

"Yeah, but I've got to figure out what to do with my business while I'm out there."

"Oh, yeah, that thing."

"Yeah, that thing."

I started a dog walking and pet sitting business just a few months ago. It seemed like a good idea at the time with having lived through the government Sequestration of 2013. I felt as though I needed something to fall back on, something that was low-cost and could get me through, should I lose my job. I shouldn't say "I felt" so much as "I've heard"

Suze Orman say it week after week on her show, and since everything she says is gospel to me, I put this plan to open a business into action. I'm supposed to conduct my first interview tomorrow. I'm licensed, insured, and ready to go, and now this fellowship. I'll have to pray a lot between now and tomorrow, but I know God will give me the answer.

"Yeah, so anyway, that's all. I'm going to head to my exercise class now."

"Okay, well, keep me posted. Hey, did you want me to come over instead and give you a real workout?"

Is he serious?

"I would love that, but I'm meeting Terry there tonight, so I can't not go."

"Okay, cool. We can hook up later this weekend."

"Sure."

"Talk to you later."

"Okay, have a good night."

I've got to pray for some serious self-love while I'm praying for direction on my business. I really do need to leave his ass alone. Funny thing, though—I called him first and hadn't yet shared this news with my parents. I'm sure there's some deep-rooted reason for this, which I'm sure Dr. Smith would love for me to explore.

"Okay, girls! One more potty break before I head out to class!"

20

The Accident

~

About ten years ago I decided to avoid the holidays as much as possible. I know this sounds crazy, since Christmas is smack in your face before Thanksgiving anymore, but I do my best to stay out of malls and places that are wildly decorated and play what is for me depressing holiday music. Until I get my Hallmark movie romance I am done with the chestnuts, open fires, sleigh bells and anything else that reminds me I am alone. And no, Dan doesn't count. Dan and his commitment-phobic ass just add to my depression each year. Besides July will be here sooner than I think, so I will just focus on getting ready to head to California.

I'm heading out for a run. Something I rarely do anymore, but I need to clear my head. I decided to go through with the interviews for my business and see if I can arrange to run the business from California. I just need a good manager. I'm sure I will be blessed with one, but right now there is so much to do. I have to run a background check on the guy I tentatively selected as a dog walker and I have to get withholding tax information filed in Maryland since that's where he lives. The good and bad of the DMV: you can do business in two states and a district, but you have to file paperwork in all of them and everyone has totally different rules.

Anyway, a clear head will help me focus this morning and get everything filed, so I can get this business moving. Running through my neighborhood sucks, as I feel a little out of place. So few people run in this area, but, oh well, it's what's on my agenda this morning. Shit! I just tripped on the curb. Man, I can't even get going for ten minutes without something happening. I'm bleeding? Really? Not bad, though, just a little cut on my wrist. Oh, shit, not my wrist! Shit, shit! Is this thing messed up? Fuck it, why am I clicking without any jerking? Wait, why can't I feel left-brainish? Damn! This thing is stuck in right-brain mode. Well, at least it's the weekend. It's all good, except I have some work to do for my small business. I'll give Monique a call and see if she can fix this thing. Or maybe it's time to take it out? But then again, she said I can't ever take it out. But surely she can fix it?

I ran for ten minutes, tripped, broke this device and now I'm back at home and staring at the forms for the business. Man, this feels hard, or rather, hard to concentrate. Maybe I need Monique sooner than next week. Maybe this shit really isn't that hard. I mean, really, what are they asking for? My IRS info, and LLC name. Really, Ava you can make things so darn hard. Just fill it out and let's move on to something else, like writing another "Adventures of Cleo and Sophie" story or finishing your inspirational novel since that's where your heart is anyway. Plus you need to purchase your plane ticket for Alabama. I hate the holidays, but love my kinfolks, so this Christmas I will hang out with them. See, you can have some logic even while you're stuck in right-brain mode.

Wait! I have a back-up! Where did I put the other remote? Heading to the bedroom where I've hidden it at the back of my dresser drawer, I stop. I don't want to fix this. I want to stay in right-brain mode. Monique said I would gradually get there anyway, so why not now? Yes, it's pretty damn quick after getting this thing, but I can't live like this anymore. I can't keep punishing myself and calling Shawshank home.

21

Back at Shawshank

~

"Ava!"

"Colonel Baker. How was your weekend?"

"Nice! I spent the entire weekend hanging with an old buddy from the Academy."

"Sounds great, sir."

"Yep. Just like the old days, only we can't drink like we used to. Had to hang it up after a few beers."

"Yeah, I can't down those Whisky Sours like I used to either."

"Ha! Really? Ava, I didn't think you drank."

"I do, sir, but mostly just wine anymore."

"Cool."

"So, I know you just got in, but the 10:00 has been moved to 8:30."

"Sure, okay. I have a 9:00, so I just won't go to the 8:30, but you've got it, right?"

"As always, sir."

"Huh? Right. Yeah. Ha! You made a joke!"

"Actually, I was speaking the truth."

"Oh, yeah. Yeah, it is the truth, too. Good call. You've always got a handle on everything. Okay, well, just give me a back brief later. I'm heading to the gym."

"Okay. Sir, I thought you had a meeting at 9:00?"

"Yep, I do, with my buddy on the ratchet ball court. It's like having a coffee meeting in the food court only we are working out while we chat."

"Of course it is, and those coffee meetings are one hundred percent productive, so yeah, I get it."

Col Baker is looking both confused and annoyed.

"Yep, that's it."

"Okay, well, enjoy your slack-off time, sir."

"Ava, really?"

"'Really' what, sir?"

"Nothing. Happy Monday, I guess."

"Ditto!"

Is right-brain supposed to make me sarcastic over time? 'Cause I like it and it's fun. I should have switched over sooner. Funny, I thought I needed left-brain at work most of the time, only switching to right for casual conversations, but hell, maybe if I am less rigid and more lighthearted I can actually survive this place.

I'm going to head to this meeting and see what in the hell comes out of my mouth. Man, this should be good!

"Ava, hey!"

"Hey, Al, what's up? How was your weekend?"

"Nice, but way too short as usual. How was yours?"

"Crazy and cool for me. I worked on my business, did some writing, and went for a run."

"No way! I thought you gave up running?"

"I did, but I decided I needed to start back. However, I only ran about ten minutes before I tripped and fell, so that put me back into 'this shit's not for me' mode."

"Oh, man. Well, hey, at least you tried."

"True."

I'm grabbing a pen off my desk and I can see Al's face. He probably has never heard me curse before, so to hear me say "shit" is shocking to him.

"I'm heading to a meeting. Be back eventually."

"Okay."

I'm practically skipping out of the office. I'm feeling free and zingy. I think I'll treat myself to breakfast after this meeting. That will be a nice change.

I get to the conference room and there they are. Lt Gen Green and Maj Gen Deeds along with a host of others looking miserable as it's another wonderful Air Force Day and yet Groundhog Day all at the same fucking time.

"Okay, folks!" says Lt Gen Green. "I got here early to get prepped for this meeting. I know many of you are thinking this a continuation of my current initiative, but it's not. Not really, anyway. This is to brainstorm on an idea I had a while back that I want to bounce off you."

Thank God, I'm just here to take notes 'cause I'm pretty sure this is going be some bullshit.

"So, I had an idea about telling our story. You know, the Air Force story. I think we are not doing a good job relaying to Congress what it is we do and why we are different from the other Services."

Wow, this is actually a real thing. I'm intrigued.

"I think the best way to get at this is to write a paper on how wonderful we are and how we do what we do and how only we can do what we do and then we write another objective paper that tells folks how we are going to do all the new things we say we can do and then we write another goal paper that gives assignments throughout our organizations on how to do what we said we'd do and then we will create a new office that will track how well we are doing everything and then we can put this out to the world. Any thoughts?"

And now we've reached Bullshitville. Next stop, What the Fuck Town.

"I've made a video that we will send out to folks on the Hill, OSD, and the Services telling them to expect this big thing from us. Let's take a look."

You have got to be shitting me.

"Hello, I'm Lieutenant General Green, and this message is for all those who lack an understanding of the Air Force and its mission."

And we just landed in What the Fuck Town! Please tell me he is not this crazy? Shouldn't a message like this, if there should even be a message like this, come from the Secretary or Chief? And who announces the coming of some shit that's not even close to being written? I'm out of here in six months.

Thank you, God, for this fellowship!

22

The Holidays

~

My whole family is originally from the South—Dothan, Alabama, to be exact—although my parents moved after my dad's retirement from the Army to Columbia, South Carolina. I love going back home to Dothan for the holidays, although there were several years when I skipped out. I was so embarrassed by getting dumped by my fiancé so he could marry his baby mamma that I just decided to forego any questions about the wedding that never took place, and before I knew it, nearly a decade had passed. When I finally did return home, it was for my grandmother's funeral.

This year is extra special to me, as I will be heading to California soon. I'm pretty sure I won't fly back for Christmas next year, so this will be my "hello and goodbye for a while" visit. I'm not really excited, though, as I would much rather spend the time with my dogs, but I'm sure my co-dependency on them needs to be weaned, so this makes for a good opportunity. I wonder why we've never discussed this in therapy?

Anyway, my flight is delayed and I am getting anxious. I don't have much of a layover in Charlotte and it's the day before Christmas Eve; there is no room for delays in arrival mainly because I am traveling first to Montgomery to visit my college and then driving on to Dothan. I can't shake this dream I had some time ago where my grandmother, whose funeral I attended nearly ten years ago, tells me she was "there," pointing to pictures of my college. I can't figure out what this means, as

I know she didn't attend my school and didn't go to college at all for that matter. I am believing that if I step foot on campus the answers will come. I'm hoping anyway.

I need something, some kind of direction for my life. One would think this fellowship would be enough, and while I am excited to spend a year away from Shawshank, I'm just in need of answers. What am I doing here and why am I just existing? Why am I not doing more, being more? I have dreams, but I don't pursue them, really. I did have a dream of a doggy daycare, but my desire to start this dog walking and pet sitting business came out of shear fear of being part of a DoD RIF (reduction in force). Since our budgets have been horrible for years, we are reducing manpower.

We discussed my plan in therapy once. Dr. Smith noted the odds of me getting fired were slim, given my tenure and my skill set and the fact that I'm a double minority. I told her she made good points and that I wish I had brought it up before I started the business. I was looking for her to tell me I could quit and shut down the business, but she didn't. I think I was hoping she'd note this was the best plan because being a business owner is a lot of work, and yes, it's also fun, and it's what I want to do, but I feel completely uneasy doing anything that actually feels right for me. I am so used to pushing through and doing what is most expected, even though I have no joy in the pursuit. I never like it, have no interest in it, yet do fairly well and sometimes excel in these things. But, doing something that gives me a rush, brings a smile to my face— well, that's just not how I was raised.

"Ladies and gentleman, flight 1525 will be delayed due to maintenance issues."

Boom. There it is. I can see all the passengers making their way up to the counter. Bump that, I'm just going to call the airline. I wonder why others don't think to do this. I guess it's the idea that the counter is right there, so logically, this approach makes sense, but there's only one maybe two people up there trying to assist everyone. I have always had much quicker service when I simply stay in my seat, dial the airline, and wait on a brief hold. Others should really give my way a try—or maybe not because then my brief hold would turn into painfully long minutes.

"Hello, how may I assist you today?"

"Hello, I am at the airport and my flight, 1525 to Charlotte has been delayed. Can you tell me if there is any chance of getting to Montgomery, Alabama today?"

"Let me look. Do you mind to hold?"

"Not at all."

"Hello, ma'am?"

"Yes?"

"Ma'am, we can get you to Charlotte, but there's no connecting flight to Montgomery."

"Okay, well, can I have a refund?"

"Are you sure you don't want to travel to Charlotte?"

"You said there are no more flights to Montgomery, correct?"

"Yes, ma'am."

"You mean, I would have to spend the night in Charlotte and fly out on Christmas Eve?"

"Yes, ma'am, but those flights are booked, so you may not be able to get to Montgomery."

"Yeah, I don't want to spend my Christmas in Charlotte."

"I can see your point."

"I'm glad you do."

"Okay, I can refund your ticket in full."

"Thank you.

"You can ask for your luggage to be pulled and given back to you."

"I only have a carry-on, so I'm good, but thank you."

"You're quite welcome, and enjoy your holidays!"

"Thank you. You, too!"

And that's that. Thank goodness I only have this carry on. I'm going to head home, get my car and get my girls! Grandma, whatever it is I need to know, I know you will reveal to me, and clearly it doesn't involve a pilgrimage to Montgomery, Alabama. At least, not at this time.

"Hello! Welcome to Pet Heaven! Oh, you're back!"

"Yes, my flight was delayed and the airline could not guarantee I would make it home for Christmas, so I decided to stay in town."

"Oh, what a sad thing. But I know two little girls who are going to be happy! I'll page for them to be sent down."

"Thank you."

While I'm waiting, I decide that I should call home and tell them not to expect me. Since my parents drive down to Dothan religiously every year for Christmas, and divide their time there between my dad's family and my mom's, I'm hoping to catch them *en route* to someone's house to avoid having to share the news with a room full of people that I'm not coming home.

"Hello? Ava?" I can barely hear him with all the noise so I know this means they're at my Aunt Ann's house.

"Hey, Dad. So, I'm not going to make it home."

"What? What happened?"

"The airline couldn't guarantee that I could make it there in time. The flight was delayed."

"Oh, okay. Well, I know you're not too upset."

"True. But I'll miss seeing everyone."

"Yeah, okay, but I know you'd rather be with the girls. Here, let me let you talk to your mom."

"Hello."

"Hey, Ma."

"Hey, Ava. You're not coming down?"

"No, there were some issues with my flight."

"Oh, did you get your money back?"

"Yes."

"Well, that's good. Ann wants to speak to you."

And now we will have a round of talk to everyone at my aunt's house in under five minutes. As I wait, the attendant comes out of the elevator with the girls.

"Here she is! Your mamma's back."

Cleo and Sophie are excited to see me. I'm good now. I'll work on my co-dependency issues another time.

"Thank you!" I say to the attendant as we gather up to leave. "See you soon! Happy Holidays!"

"What, now?" says my aunt on the phone.

"Oh, I'm picking up the girls from boarding. I was speaking to the attendant."

"Oh, well, honey, we gonna let you go, but you be sure to make it here next year."

"Well, Ruby, I will be in California," I say to my aunt, "so I was thinking how nice it would be if ya'll came out to see me and have Christmas at the beach."

"Honey, no, you know most of us don't do no flying, especially Ann."

"Well, this would be a good time to start."

"Nope, not happening! You be good now, okay."

"Okay, tell everyone else I said hello."

"Okay, baby. Love you."

"Love you, too."

Well, that felt bad and good. Sadly, my family is so used to me blowing them off for the dogs, they really don't bat an eye anymore if I don't show up. I think that should concern me, but it doesn't. Anyway, I have no food at home. I need to get these girls home and then hit the grocery store.

23

A Man for Christmas?

~

Surprisingly the grocery store is not packed with last-minute shoppers, but it is the day before Christmas Eve, so maybe I beat the rush. What do I want this year? Traditional. Yep, I may not be in Alabama, but I'm going to make a southern Christmas dinner. But, I'm going to cheat and get this rotisserie chicken and these rolls and these precooked sides. Can I cook? Yes, I can go to town on some dishes when I feel like it. Do I cook? Rarely anymore. I find it depressing to cook for just me; as the years pass and I'm still single, I cook less and less.

Why is Dan calling me? Normally I get a generic holiday text that I'm sure he sends to everyone in his contacts.

"Hey."

"Ava-Flava, what's up?"

"Nothing, just grocery shopping."

"What for? Shouldn't you be on a plane?"

"Yeah, but I'm not. Are you enjoying your family?"

"I didn't go home."

"Really?"

"Yeah. So, we're both in town, huh?"

"Yep, looks that way."

"Do you want me to come over?"

"Sure."

"Okay, I'll swing by tomorrow tonight. Make sure you're shaved up for me."

"Of course."

Why, God? Why? How can I even muster up an ounce of excitement about this? But maybe this is a sign. We are both in town for Christmas. Surely this means something? That we will spend the holiday together?

The day has progressed nicely. I've made my makeshift Christmas dinner early out of hunger and boredom, and I've gotten ready for Dan. Please God, let him see something special about us tonight. Please let this mean something, that we are both in town for Christmas. Please let this be my first enjoyable Christmas with a man, please.

THE DOORBELL'S RINGING but I'm not moving. I don't have to dig deep in my heart to know this is not what I want it to be. Oh well, let's just get things moving.

"Hey."

"Hey. What took you so long to open the door?"

"I don't know.'

"Huh?"

"Yeah, I don't know."

"Okay, well, this is for you."

It's a bottle of Shiraz. I hate red wine, as it gives me a headache. Something I've never bothered to share with Dan.

"Thanks. Why don't you open it?"

"Okay. So, how was your day?"

"Good. How was yours?"

"Good. Didn't do anything; just another day."

"I guess."

I have absolutely no feelings for this man. That's a lie, but I think I'm doing good at suppressing them. No, actually, I'm not.

Dan hands me a glass of wine.

"Thank you."

"This is nice, both of us here for the holiday."

"Yeah, it's nice. So, why did you decide to stay?"

"Because my family is a piece of shit."

"Oh, that seems unlikely."

"No, it's true. You know I've told you about all of them."

"Yes, you have, but I didn't deduce 'piece of shit' from what you've said. They seem like everybody else's family, a little crazy, but that's normal."

Dan suffers from something in the realm of childhood neglect and mother hatred. I've never seen anyone hate their mother so much. I'm sure there is much more than he will ever share about her, but from what he's shared, she seems to have never cared for him. He is the younger of two boys and apparently his brother is the only one his mother ever wanted. She told him once he was only alive because the birth control didn't work, and another time that, had she only had his brother, she would have left his father, but she didn't think she could make it on her own with two kids, so she was forced to stay. I can only imagine this would fuck with a person's psyche. I've told Dan on multiple occasions that he should look into therapy, but he just blows me off.

"You think I'm exaggerating about my childhood."

"Not at all, but I think you should finally work through your issues and move past all of it. It's clearly the reason you are an ass most of the time."

"Thanks a lot, Ava. Merry Christmas to you, too."

"If you would accept it, my gift to you would be a session with Dr. Smith."

"Don't hold back on your thoughts tonight."

"Look, it's nothing I haven't said before, but really, you need to get your shit together. You're forty-five years old."

"I know how old I am."

"Then get your shit together. Life is short. People die every damn day. Fix your shit before it's too late."

I love how I can tell Dan this, but fuck up every week after my session with Dr. Smith. I'm enjoying right-brain. I don't think I'm ever going to have Monique fix this thing. I feel free to say whatever the hell is on my mind, and it's like the thoughts of wisdom and wisecracks just flow.

"Yeah, I hear you. But right now I need you to suck my dick."

"Not at all feeling like that right now, so, no."

"Excuse me?"

"I should have told you that on the phone. This thing with us is whack, and I'm not in the mood to even remotely pretend tonight. You know what I want? I want to be with someone who loves me and respects me. I want a fucking romantic Christmas; a freaking Hallmark movie Christmas, not some going through the motions of a relationship with you that leads to emotionless sex."

"Damn, Ava! I'm out!"

"Wait, no. You shouldn't leave like this."

"Ava, I don't know what the fuck is going on with you right now, but I'm not hanging around for you to talk shit about me on Christmas Eve."

"I'd call it talking truth."

"Whose truth?"

"Mine, yours. Look Dan, we are both fucked up. The only difference is I am trying to get my shit together. I can't understand why in the hell you want to keep living like this. Mad at the world and your mamma all the damn time."

"Yeah, well, black men don't go to therapy, Ava, and actually, not many black women do, either. You ought to be praying about your issues instead of paying someone to hang out in their office every week."

"I do pray, but do you? All you do is tell me these horror stories about your childhood and then say, 'and that's why I'm fucked up.' You don't want my advice and that's cool. I can be a listening ear, but you do need to work this shit out. Think about it this way. You could live another fifty years. Do you want to carry around all this shitload of anger for another fifty fucking years?"

"I'm used to it."

"Well, I bet your load would be a lot lighter if you let this shit go once and for all."

"Yeah, I guess."

Dan looks pathetic. I'm glad I finally got that shit off my chest, though. I just hope it sinks in.

"So, what's on TV?" he says finally. "You got like a thousand channels."

"Yeah, I do need to reduce my cable bill."

"Oh snap! *Friday*! And it's at the beginning. Let's watch this. I love this movie."

"Me, too."

Who am I kidding? None of this is sinking in. This fool is just trying to keep the peace to get to have sex tonight. I'll watch this movie, but there will be no sex. Really? He has the nerve to want to cuddle. Does he think I'm that gullible? Probably because I act that way all the damn time. So damn desperate for his time and attention, and he knows it. He plays right into my insecurities. I should tell him to leave, but it is Christmas Eve. But definitely no sex.

24

Christmas Day

~

Thank you, God, for another day of living, blessings, love, and support, and thank you, God, for sending your son to this earth to die for our sins.

I should get up and let the babies out to potty before Dan wakes up.

I can't believe I have absolutely no backbone, no self-love, nothing. But, I'm not alone on Christmas Day. Then again, I am.

"Come on, girls. Let's go potty."

25

Four-Inch-Heels

~

I have been in pain since I tripped back in the fall and broke this device. My foot now looks strange and I've finally surrendered to seeing my podiatrist.

Dr. Clark is smiling at me.

"Ava. First, Happy New Year."

"Happy New Year to you, too."

"Ava, didn't we go through this very thing a few years ago?"

"Yes, but I think I was in disbelief that I could actually break my other foot."

"Well, looking at this X-Ray I'd say you can let go of that disbelief. And you still work at the Pentagon, yes?"

"Yes."

"And, pull those shoes out of your bag."

I hop off the chair and pull out a pair of four-inch pumps.

"I know what you're thinking, but I only wear them in the building."

"Only in a building with a concrete floor. You know this is not helping and it's also stressing your right foot that we repaired five years ago."

"I know, but I have to look a certain way."

"You can be quite the professional in a pair of flats."

"True, but I'm also very short."

"Okay, well, for this current issue. Surgery, of course, and soon is recommended."

"Sure, okay."

"I have a few dates coming up. Looks like February eleventh is the next available."

"Sounds great, that's my birthday."

"You want to have surgery on your birthday?"

"Sure, this way I get a couple of weeks off as a birthday present."

"Alright. I'll have the girls schedule this for you and in the meantime, try, if you can, to stay out of heels."

"I'll work on it."

"Today, you can start working on it."

"Oh, yeah, sure. Yep, today."

"Okay, I'll see you in a couple of weeks."

"Cool, see you."

I'm excited to get two weeks off for my birthday, unconventional as this may be. I think it's pretty damn clever, though I think most people would just take time off from work and not need the surgery as an excuse. But, I'm certainly not like most people. I can't wait to break the news to Col Baker.

I'M NOT A fan of driving to Shawshank, but I do it when I have doctor's appointments. The drive isn't as bad after the morning rush, so this should be a smooth ride in. I wonder who I will ask to help me this time, though I hate bothering any of my friends. Dan could help, but the senator he works for has been spending a lot of time back home gearing up for campaign season, so I'm sure he'll be out of town supporting him. I think I'll just take the bus and have a car service bring me home. I'll give it a little bit more thought, but yep, that seems like the best plan.

26

Back at Shawshank

~

"Ava! Just in time!"

"Just in time for what?" Al has a really huge grin on his face.

"Just in time to have missed staff meeting!"

"Oh, darn. I'm sure it was very informative."

"Oh, it is was. We spent the entire time discussing the new Rainbow Sheets Lieutenant General Green wants to use."

"The what?"

"The Rainbow Sheets. You know how we have Snowflakes and BLINDS? Well, we now have the Rainbow."

Snowflakes and BLINDS (can't even recall what the hell BLIND stands for) are brief descriptions of an issue we add to a package for our leadership. They are a longer version of a BLUF (bottom line up front), but shorter than a Staff Summary Sheet. All of these basically do the same thing. They provide a short background and recommendation for senior leadership. So what the fuck is a Rainbow?

"So, Al, what the fuck is a Rainbow?"

"Language, Ms. Ava. Really? But, glad you asked. A Rainbow—that's R.A.N.B.O—is a Ready Analysis Needed Before Opinion. In other words, it's going to be our short background and recommendation provided with each package up to Lieutenant General Green."

"That's the same thing as a Snowflake or a BLIND or a BLUF. Oh, but wait you said 'analysis'—we get to state our opinion?"

"Of course not. It's the same thing with a different acronym."

"Of course."

"Anyway, the front office has sent out the template for it and we need to start using it ASAP."

"Got it." I can't wait to start this fellowship in a few months and take a break from this foolishness. "Thanks for the heads up. I've got a package to send up today, so I'd better check my inbox for the RANBO template!"

"Yeah, you better. And how was the doctor's visit?"

"Good. Need surgery."

"Dang. That's too bad. Wait, you said 'good'?"

"Yep. I scheduled it for my birthday next month."

"What the hell for?"

"To take some time off."

"Most people just take leave."

"Yeah, but two birds, one stone, right?"

"I guess. As long as you can admit that's just some weird ass shit to do."

"Ava!" I somehow thought I'd get to get my coffee before Col Baker and I had words today.

"Hey, sir."

"Ava, got to discuss this RANBO deal with you."

"Al just filled me in."

"Oh, cool, thanks, Al."

"Sure thing, sir."

Al is grinning from ear to ear as he leaves me with Col Baker.

"So, I think we should do a RANBO to talk about killing this new 'what we do' initiative."

"I didn't gather from Al that was the point of the RANBO, sir."

"No, but if we use this new thing, Lieutenant General Green will be impressed, and that may help with convincing him to stop this before it gets out of control."

"You mean writing a new strategy for the Air Force?"

"Yeah, exactly. This is not going to go well."

"Why is that, sir? Because it's a lot of work and nobody's going to read it?"

"Ava, no! Of course people will read it."

"Probably. The media and bloggers will, but not those who actually support the mission. They will see it as the Headquarters once again telling them how to do their job that either no one who will write this thing will know about or will not have done in twenty years. They won't read it. I never read it when I was at the depot. Heck, I couldn't even tell you who the Secretary and Chief were for the longest time. But, I would manage parts of the depot like a boss and get shit done and aircraft back to their home base, but nope I didn't read the Mother Ship's strategy to accomplish my job."

"Thank you for that insight, but I'm thinking because we are less than two years shy of a new administration, and it's been nearly a decade since we wrote a strategy, we should just stick to our five issues and press with a new strategy after the election."

"The election that is a year and a half away?"

"Yes."

"Okay, well I don't agree with you for that reason, but I do think it's not going to aid in accomplishing the mission."

"What? Why would you say that?"

"Because no one who really needs to do the work will be identified in this thing. And those who read it won't do anything. We will expend hundreds of man-hours writing this thing with all its annexes and metrics and it will be overkill to MAJCOMs. Trust me, before coming here, I worked at a depot where we successfully, and sometimes unsuccessfully, did our job and we never read or cared about the Air Force strategy. We just did the damn thing. We spend more time telling the field what it needs to do when the field is functioning just fine, and when they do need our assistance, we don't seem to really help them. Isn't that why we are here at the HAF (Headquarters Air Force)? To support them?"

"You are being quite colorful about this, but I don't think we can kill this with your blatant honesty. But since we are on the same page about it not needing to get done, let's see how to make that happen."

"Yeah, so, I'm having surgery next month."

"Oh?"

"Yeah, I'll be out for two weeks starting on the eleventh."

"Okay. Is it necessary?"

"No."

"Really?"

"Yes, of course, it's necessary. Why would you ask me that?"

"Umm, I really don't know. You are being really fiery lately."

"I guess. I'm probably reaching the stage of being jaded."

"Jaded?"

"Too many years here in Shawshank."

"Shawshank? You mean the building?"

"Yep."

"You do need to get out of here. This fellowship is going to do you a world of good. Some time out of the Beltway is just what you need. You do excellent work, Ava. But, you do a lot and we do lean on you for way too much. It's a good thing you're getting this break soon."

"Well, thanks for that, sir. I appreciate it."

"Sure thing. I'm off for a coffee meeting."

Well, that was shocking, but I think it's me in right-brain overload that's doing this. I'm so blunt lately. I really need to tell Monique, but I am just loving this mode. I really don't see the harm in going on like this a little bit longer. I'll let her know in a couple of weeks. I should fix it prior to heading out to California, and I do feel bad for lying to her and telling her all is well every time she does my hair.

Surgery Day

~

I am not a morning person. Waking up at 5:00 a.m. to get to the hospital was painful, but I did it. I hope today is a breeze and I am home and resting by noon. I'm glad I stuck to my decision to take the bus to the hospital and use a car service for the ride home. I'm just not in the mood for anyone right now. I first learned of Wings on Call a few years ago when I needed an endoscopy for an ulcer I had developed. I was hesitant to take the time from work for the procedure and told the doctor during my initial exam that I simply did not have anyone who could take me home afterward. I thought surely this would end the discussion, and I'd be one of those antacid popping people for a few years and readdress the issue at a later date. Plus, I'd seen on Dr. Oz how Kefir milk could assist in the healing of an ulcer, so issue resolved, I thought, but my doctor didn't go for it. He told me the hospital was affiliated with companies that provided home health care that include car services for patients. While the hospital would not allow its patients to take a cab, bus, or the train home, these home health care companies were vetted and verified for use. My thought at the time was, damn, but in the end, a lovely older lady wearing a bright red cowboy hat arrived after my endoscopy and took me home with no problems. Now, here I am using them again, all because I don't like to lean on my friends for support.

However, I do wish the switch on this device was working because left-brain would be great for today, to just march on through this, but, oh well, right, it is. I really should call Monique and have her fix this thing. While I'm off for two weeks after this surgery, I may give her a call. I'm still lying to her, telling her it's great. I'm worried, though, she's going to ask to do some kind of check or tune up and find out this thing's been broken for months now. But so far, she just asks, "How's it going?" and I say, "Fine." Since I'm stuck in right-brain mode, it's easy enough for her not to notice, since that's how I would normally behave at the salon. The question is, why won't I tell her it's broke. The answer is, right-brain mode is the shit, and I'm loving it. So what if it's tanking my career and half-assed relationship?

As I enter the surgery center I see a cheerful looking nurse. She's beaming from ear to ear and it's only 6:00 a.m.

"Good morning. Please sign in."

"Good morning."

Looking around, there doesn't appear to be a packed house today. Hopefully they can process me and get me prepped quickly. I really think I'm supposed to be more concerned than this. It's just my foot, and I'm not worried about the procedure, but I am wondering about the fact that I have no feelings one way or the other about being here alone. Or, maybe if I'm thinking about it, then I do actually have feelings. Maybe I am feeling some kind of way about having no support, or rather, not asking for support. I have a ton of friends who would gladly have brought me here and taken me home. I have helped them out on many occasions with similar situations, but for me to be the one asking for help, well, I just can't or don't. I feel as though I'm putting people out. I should probably bring this up in therapy, but for now, I'll just note Wings on Call on this form as my "who to call" post-surgery.

"Ava McClure."

Great, let's get this thing started.

"Hello, my name is Pam and I will be your nurse today."

"Hello, Pam."

Pam appears to be very pleasant, but it is 6:00 a.m. and I'm her first patient. I'm sure her jolly demeanor may alter by 10:00.

"I'm going to have you change into this gown and then I'll be right back."

"Okay." Two weeks off is going to be really nice. Maybe I'll get a lot of writing done. That would be nice.

"Okay, I'm going to take your vitals and then hook you up to your IV. Your doctor is running a little behind this morning, as he ran into some complications in his first surgery."

"Really? I didn't know surgeries started before 6:00 a.m."

"Yes, but he should be wrapping up soon."

Pam looks like Carol Brady, haircut and all. I wonder if people ever tell her this. She is gentle with everything she does. I wanted to be a nurse when I was a child until I was saw a man with his knee cap shot off in the emergency room. After that I was sure I wouldn't do well in the profession, plus I had a fear of the dead back then; by age ten, I was on to something else.

"So, who should I call to come sit with you while you wait?"

"Oh, no one. I'm here alone."

"Alone?" Pam is covering me with blankets. She is practically tucking me into this bed.

"Yes, I had a friend drop me off and a car service is picking me up. It's noted in my registration paperwork." (No need for Pam to know I took the bus here. It's bad enough I'm using a car service to take me home.)

"Oh, my. I'm sorry no one is here for you today."

"It's okay."

"Are you okay? Are you warm enough?"

"Yes, I'm good, thank you."

"Well, I'll leave you to rest and I'll check back with you soon."

"Okay."

I'VE BEEN SITTING here for two hours and I have to pee. I hate to bother Pam but I can't hold it anymore. Then she arrives.

"Hey, sweetie, your doctor is wrapping up and will be in in just a few minutes."

"Thanks, Pam. I hate to bother you, but I have to use the restroom."

"Oh, of course, dear! Here, let me help you up. Now be sure to walk slowly with the IV."

"Okay, thank you."

I'm starting to feel lonely as I wheel my IV down the hall. I don't know why I never ask anyone for help. Taking the bus to a surgery when I live in a city with a dozen friends who could help me? They are going to jump down my throat when they find out I did this. I really do need to bring this up with Dr. Smith. I'm certain I'll never be done with therapy. I'll be ninety-five in a nursing home, still having weekly sessions.

"You made it back okay. That's good!"

Pam is way too nice.

"Yep."

"Let me help you back in the bed."

"Thank you."

Pam smiles and closes the curtain.

I'm again warmly tucked under the covers. It feels good, safe. Maybe getting tucked in to bed brings about some psychological childhood memory stuff. I didn't grow up with the most nurturing set of parents, but my sister and I did get tucked in to bed every night, and my dad would tell us some wild ass story from his childhood. It was then I felt loved and part of the family nucleus. It was short-lived each day, but it was something.

The curtain opens again.

"Ava."

"Hello, Dr. Clark."

"Ready for some surgery?"

"Sure."

"Okay, well, you know the routine, same as a few years ago. We'll reset your foot today and you'll come in the office next week for me to examine you."

"Yep."

"Okay, well, let's get going."

Dr. Clark leaves, and another doctor enters.

"Hello, I'm Dr. Edwards. I'm your anesthesiologist."

"Hello."

"I'm going to get you going now and you will probably be asleep before we get to the operating room."

"Sounds good."

I'm always intrigued when I go under for a surgery (I've had a few, plus the endoscopy), how I go from relaxed to sleepy to awake with screws in my foot or mesh netting in my stomach (hernia repair) or stitches in my breast (cyst removed, benign, thank you, God!).

THERE'S NOISE AND laughter, but I'm just not ready to open my eyes. I do love the restfulness of being put to sleep. There's no better feeling than this. If only I could wake up this restful every morning. I bet this is how Michael Jackson felt, why he wanted his propofol. Rest on, MJ, though you are dearly missed.

"There you are!"

I'm barely seeing Pam as my eyelids are very heavy, but I'm too awake to go back to sleep.

"Hi."

"Hello, honey. Everything went well. Dr. Clark will be by in a few minutes."

"Okay."

"Ava. Everything went well. I did though use three pins for this foot. We only used one in the other, but this one was a little worse off."

"Oh, okay."

"Take your pain meds, use your crutches, and see me in a week, and happy birthday!"

"Thank you! Sounds great, see you in a week."

Pam is looking very confused as she hands me a small tray with graham crackers and ginger ale. "It's your birthday?" she says.

"Yes.

"Who has surgery on their birthday?"

"Someone who wants two weeks off for their birthday present."

"Smart."

"Thank you."

"Who should we call to pick you up?"

"The Wings on Call car service is picking me up."

"Yes, right. I know you told me this earlier, but my goodness, it's your birthday! No family or friends?"

"Everyone was super busy and this works out just fine."

"Okay, I'll check your file and give them a call. I know we allow for these services, but, well, I have to say it again, it's your birthday.

"Thanks."

I give Pam a faint smile, not because this saddens me, but because I think it would disturb her more if I didn't show some concern about this myself. There's a good chance I'll never mention this to Dr. Smith, though I'm sure I should.

Pam returns and says, "Okay, dear. They are on their way."

"Thanks so much, and thanks for your help today."

"You are most welcome. Oh, just one last thing. Do you know how to use the crutches?"

"Oh, yes. I've had them before."

"Oh, great then. I'll leave you to get dressed."

I feel great and I'm getting out of here by noon, so no complaints from me. I had Dr. Clark's office call in my prescriptions last week and picked them up prior to today, so this should be a breeze to get home and back to my babies. I recall from a few years ago that I didn't need the pain meds, and I hope the same will be true this time.

"Alright dear, your car is here." Pam has returned with a wheelchair and her perky smile.

"Great, thanks."

Pam has wheeled me to the front of the surgery center entrance and I see my driver, an elderly white man who appears to be in his mid-seventies. She is helping me into the car and whispering in my ear, though I am not sure why the whispering.

"Now remember to take it easy and rest and happy birthday!"

"Thank you, and I will!"

"Hello, ma'am. How are you today?" says the driver.

"I'm good, thank you."

"I hope you're feeling well after your surgery, or as well as you can be."

"Oh, I'm doing great actually."

Awkward small talk with a stranger while still a little high from the anesthesia will be interesting, but it's not my first rodeo as I used a car service a few years back when I had to have an endoscopy. Long story, but the short of it is, don't take twenty pain killers in five hours hoping to cure anything, as it only results in an ulcer. Also, fortunately the hospital is only about ten minutes from my house.

"Well, here we are."

Yes, we are, indeed, and at this very moment I'm remembering how the last time it took Sheryl and me a long time to get up these stairs. There are about sixteen stairs from street level to the front door of the house I live in. My driver is doing all he can to help me, but not touch me (for liability reasons), while I'm working my way from the car to the first step. This is going to be rough and I'm sure he's not allowed to go past this point, again, for liability reasons.

"I can help you carry your bags."

"Thank you, that would be great."

It's at least something. I can do this. I just need to use my good right leg and hold on to this rail and hop my butt up sixteen steps. I've got to have that much in me after pole workouts and FREAKAZOID! Okay, not bad. First five down, now eleven more to go. Go, Ava, go! And hurry because I'm sure this dude is feeling all kinds of awkward as he holds my stuff and stays a good five feet away from me. Just a few more hops. Alrighty, and done!

"Thanks, again."

"You're welcome, ma'am, and thank *you*!"

I take it he's pleased with my twenty dollar tip. I guessed on the amount. I do 20 percent for pretty much everything unless you're an ass. I even tip 20 percent at the nail salon, which I know most people think is insane, but I do it anyway.

"Hey, babies! Who needs to go potty? Okay, potty break and then nap time!"

THIS DAMN PHONE scared the shit out of me. I was in a deep sleep after I let the dogs out to potty.

"Hello?"

"Ava-Flava! Happy Birthday!"

"Thanks!"

"How was your day? Did you do anything fun?"

"I had my surgery today."

"What? Did you mention that?"

"Yes."

"Damn, Ava. I don't think you did."

"You're out of town, so you couldn't have helped. No worries."

"Yeah, but this dude could have come back home by himself. He doesn't need me here, he needs me back on The Hill. Plus, that's why he has staffers, not his Chief of Staff. Anyway, I could have helped you out like I did before."

A couple of years back Dan took me to have a cyst removed from my uterine wall. The same day, just hours after he brought me back home, he had one of his fits and stopped speaking to me for months. Not to sound like a victim, but really? This man got upset because I gave him a thank you card with an I OWE U book for cute little things like "cook dinner" or "have sex." He wanted to know what he was supposed to do with something like that, as the cute little book didn't match his home décor. I said it wasn't a coffee table book and he didn't have to display it. He said it made him feel like I was trying to claim his space, leave a mark in his home. I said if we are only dating each other, then whom was I leaving a mark for? He then proceeded to yell at me, so I hung up on him. I guess in hindsight, that one was on me, but I still think he overreacted.

I have always had my suspicions, though, that there were others. I guess I just find it hard to believe that there are other women as desperate as I am that they'd have anything to do with an asshole like Dan. I'm beginning to think I'm wrong about this, but then again, he's always available and always answers when I call. I guess, then, maybe I'm the main chick and not the side chick. It would explain, though, why I got chlamydia once, though he swears he was clean and clearly I got it from public toilet seat or something, never mind that I had been recently tested for and cleared of all STDs. This happened after one of our splits. I wasn't upset with the chlamydia, just with the lying. If he got it while we were apart, then okay, except next time get yourself checked. But I will say, when we are together, I've never gotten anything before or after that one time. So, maybe there are no others, and if that's the case, then indeed, I am the only fool dealing with him.

"Thanks, that's sweet. Why don't you stop by when you get back? I'm off for two weeks."

"Yeah, that sounds great. Well, I'd better go take care of this dude."

"Okay, thanks for the call."

"Sure thing. Goodnight."

"Goodnight."

Well, now it's time to see what this new TV show, *Empire*, is all about. Everyone is talking about it, and I'm lost in my world of dog business and writing. But, I've got two weeks at home and On Demand, so let's see what I've been missing.

28

Back at Shawshank

~

Two weeks off has been great and *Empire* is the bomb (do people still say that)? I hate, though, that I must return to my reverse work-release program today. I'm feeling nauseated as I enter my office.

"She's back! Ava, how was your time off? Are you all healed up?"

Col Baker is beaming from ear to ear, thankful that his workhorse is back, I'm sure.

"Not quite, sir." I'm gazing down at the boot cast on my foot.

"Oh, yeah, how long with that thing?"

"About six weeks."

"Damn, that sucks."

"Sure does, but at least I get to drive and park close to the building."

"Should you be walking that far with that thing? There is no such thing as parking close to this building, at least not for us sausage-making folks."

"It's close enough."

I'm saying this and already feeling the effects of the long walk from the parking lot. Last time I had this type of surgery, I was off for seven weeks, but I can't afford that much time off now. I have a lot to do prior to heading out to California in a few months. I must admit I'm getting more and more excited about this fellowship. I really believe time out of Shawshank is just what I need.

I decided while I was off to just focus on clearing out here and doing the same for my place. I'm going to toss away most of my belongings and start fresh when I return next year. And that includes my work files. I hoard everything, every email, every document I've ever printed. It's not necessary, and I do believe it's the result of my scatted mind.

I also need to feel sorry for whomever Col Baker deems the lucky recipient of my workload. I do have interesting assignments, though, so they'll have that going for them—just the extra burden of doing their job plus Col Baker's.

But, that's not for me to worry about as I am just going to set my sights on Santa Monica. The idea of living there is amazing, and I am truly blessed. I want to savor every moment of this experience, and to do that, I don't need to feel rushed or stressed about getting ready to head west. I know it's only March, but I am hell-bent on making this a remarkable experience. So, clear the house and clear Shawshank.

PART III

{FREEDOM}

29

Oatmeal and Tongs

~

The month of March flew by with me obtaining my second client for my dog walking business and the purchase of a new car, a Range Rover Evoque, though I really wanted a Jeep Wrangler Unlimited. I allowed myself to be convinced that a forty-two-year-old woman heading off for a prestigious fellowship in Southern California doesn't drive a jeep; she upgrades to something with class and style. All the BS talk of Dan. I've owned a Honda Prelude and a Toyota 4 Runner and, well, I'm just that type of girl. I was a tomboy growing up, and I like sport cars, trucks, and jeeps; nonetheless, I now own a cute little baby Range. I don't know why I feel the need to be in Dan's league. He has two incomes as a Chief of Staff and a Reservist. He and his Audi are great together. I should have bought my jeep or maybe even a Honda. But, this is a cool little car and has more features than I'll even figure out how to operate.

It's April and it's cold. I hate the weather here and I can't wait to reside in sunny SoCal soon. Tonight is date night at Dan's. He's excited because I am coming over to see him and it's not after a therapy session. This means I'm making time for him. He loves to pretend that he's indifferent, but he's really not. As much as he likes to be an ass, I can see clearly into his soul and I know he wants to be in loving relationship. I just wish I knew what made him this way, other than his dysfunctional relationships with his mother. Was it one bad relationship or many that built this wall around him? I get it, though. I joke that I don't just have a wall, but a mote and alligators swimming around me. I guess that's why we've made it this long. Two broken people who really aren't trying to do better. I think, though, he fears therapy will someday allow me to walk away, but it doesn't make him act like any less of an ass.

"Ava, hey, let me just drop this in the shoot."

"Okay."

"How was your day? How's your new car?"

"Good and good. How was your day?"

"Shitty. But I turned in my resignation today."

"What?"

"Yeah. It's time to quit this bullshit and do something else."

"Wow! Well, that's great. Are you going to do the real estate thing?"

"Most definitely. I just got my license again, so it's on! You should do it, too. Didn't you once have your license back in Oklahoma?"

"Yeah, I did, but I never did anything with it

"So, do something with it now. Damn girl, you've had your real estate license and you have a dog walking business—you have an entrepreneurial spirit in you. At least hustle and get your side gig strong."

"I am. I just interviewed a bunch of people for dog walking positions. I've decided to hire a manager and run the business from California."

"Cool. That's what I'm talking about."

"So, what's with all these pictures?"

Laid out across the kitchen island are a handful of pictures. I see a running theme of Dan and a baby.

"Oh, just organizing some stuff. This is me with my niece when she was little, and this is me with my best friend's daughter. She loves me. All kids love me."

"That's great." (I would have never guessed.)

This is a confusing and awkward moment. I'm not sure where this conversation is going. Dan is now reaching in the cabinet.

"I was at Whole Foods the other day and I remember you saying you were running low on oatmeal so I bought you some."

"Oh, gee, wow…that's incredibly thoughtful of you. Thanks."

"Sure, and I was at Bed Bath and Beyond and I got you these. Pretty nice, huh?"

Dan is waving cooking tongs at me.

"Yeah, those are nice. Thanks."

I also notice the television is on and the movie playing is *Pretty Woman*. I'm not sure what's happening.

"You know I'm making your favorite."

"I will miss your steaks."

"Yeah, you will. What else are you going to miss?"

Oh lord, why?

"Oh, I'm not sure. I can't think of anything else."

"Really?"

Please let him keep his penis in his pants. I want sex, but I want this to feel more like dinner than a booty call. But perhaps that's what it is. He's purchased oatmeal and cookware. Maybe this is how he says, "I love you."

"I can think of a few things, like, oh, say, our great discussions on politics. And who is going to watch bizarre documentaries with me?"

Oh, thank god, he's not trying to have sex…but what the hell is he doing? What is he talking about?

"Well, there's this cool invention called the 'phone.' We can still talk, and we do that a lot now, but yeah, you'll be on your own to watch *The Secret Life of Beavers*."

"We'll figure it out. Ready for dinner? I can rewind this and we can watch it from the beginning."

"Really, you want to watch it from the beginning?"

"For you, yes."

"Okay, then I'm taking you up on that!"

This is the best date we've ever had. Why is it happening right before I leave? Dan and I are not in a relationship and he's made that very clear throughout the years, so it's not a date. Stop with the poor Ava crap. He's just being Dan. Doing everything like you are together and bailing as soon as it starts to feel like you are together. Happy with your "we're only sleeping with each other for safety" reasons, but let's not confuse that with dating exclusively and being in a committed relationship. Or, "here, you can wear my sweats after you came over in nothing but a skimpy negligee and a trench coat," and cuddle on the couch and watch TV. Just enjoy this moment, Ava, and let the rest of this shit go.

"How did I do with the steaks?"

"Fabulous, as always!"

We are gazing at each other like two people in a movie about to be drawn in for their first kiss. He's so fucking sexy. I wish he were an unattractive slob, but then again, he would then never have gotten my attention.

Dan's tongue is deep inside my mouth, our breathing is faint. The last time this happened was on our first date five years ago. Since then all he wants is for me perform oral sex and then move straight to doggy-style fucking. Maybe he really does love me. Maybe there is more here than a strange pseudo-relationship/friends-with-benefits thing. He's now kissing my neck. His breath is heavy, strong. We are undressing each other and can barely make it to the couch. He's straddling my naked body and my legs are parted for his entry. The weight of his body on me feels delightful and strange as our status quo position, doggy-style, has been replaced with missionary style. My legs wrap around his waist and our bodies grind in a beautiful rhythm. We kiss and moan and he moves to position my body from lying down to sitting up. His head is between my thighs and his tongue is making my body quiver. My legs are shaking uncontrollably. I'm looking down at him with pleasure and confusion. Now he's picking me up and sliding back inside me. With my legs wrapped around his body he carries me to the bedroom. We are kissing as he lowers me on the bed. Surely he's ready for doggy-style, but no, or not quite. He turns me over, but lies on top of me. With all of his weight on me he grinds heavy and deep. I can't help but grind with him, whirling my ass in rhythm with his thrusts—again this easy rhythm finds its way inside me. I'm carefree, unworried about my performance, just in the moment.

This is amazing.

This is real sex. This is five years in the making.

One more thrust and he explodes. Why in the hell is this happening two months before I leave?

IT'S MISTING AS Dan walks me to my car. It's a chilly April night, and for me, spring in the District is nothing shy of winter; it's bitter cold and miserable.

I always park in a parking garage across from his building. I've only once gotten a parking spot on the street in all these years, so I don't bother to even look around his area. I just make a beeline to this garage and don't think about the price for parking.

"Ava, damn, you wore me out tonight."

"Yeah, you had me breathless, too."

"That's what I like about us. We have such great chemistry."

"Yeah, we do."

I don't know why we always say this when, until tonight, it was such a lie. Or, maybe only a lie to me. To me chemistry means more than connecting sexually. For Dan, I'm guessing that's not the case.

Regardless, we're still the same two broken people trying to hold on to something that's the closest they've been to any kind of a good relationship, and yet it is light years from anything anyone with good sense would desire.

"Really, you've already got the dog seats in this thing?"

"My need to take the dogs places didn't disappear when I got this car."

"True, but you kill me." Dan's laugh is kind and warm. It's usually critical and sarcastic.

"Call me when you get home. This weather is tricky. It seems like it's not really doing much, but the roads are still wet and slick."

"Okay, I will. I do hate this time of year here. It's cold and wet but not winter cold. You know?"

Dan is smiling at me like I'm a cute little kid asking a ridiculous question.

"Yeah, my friend was over the other day and we were talking about the spring season here and she, um, he was agreeing that it sucks."

"Okay, well, I'd better go. Goodnight."

Dan gives me a peck on the lips, but avoids looking at me. I'm sure he's kicking himself for his slip up. I'm hurt and shocked, but since the evening was perfect, I'm just going to get in my car and go home.

"Want a ride out of here?"

"Yeah, sure. I don't know why you always have to park this far down."

"I'm not the best driver, so I like to park with as few cars around as possible."

Dan gazes around and sees the three cars on this level of the garage. "Well, you accomplished that."

"Thank you for always walking me to my car."

"You're most welcome, as always."

He smiles at me and walks around to the passenger side, and I get in and start the car. Our drive up to the top is quiet. I want to blurt out, who is this "she" you mentioned, but I know if I do, it will ruin the night. I reach the garage exit and stop the car. Dan leans over and kisses me on the cheek.

"I had a wonderful evening, Ava."

"Me, too. Goodnight."

"Goodnight."

Dan gets out and closes the door. I wait as he crosses in front of my car and then jaywalks across the street. Let it go, Ava. Let it go. Maybe I'm reading more into this than there is? I've often slipped up and said he/she. Did he look caught? Now that I think about it, he didn't. He just made an innocent mistake. Let it go, Ava, let it go. But he gave me cooking tongs. I never said I needed cooking tongs. Oatmeal, yes, but not tongs. Maybe she said she needed them. Maybe he got us confused. I should have mentioned that earlier when he gave them to me. Maybe then I would have noticed something off, or maybe he would have been more on point to not slip up and say "she" just now.

I'VE MADE IT home and I'm still stuck on she/he.

"Hey, girls! Let's go potty!"

Let it go, Ava, let it go. Things are great with Dan right now and you are trying to mess it up. Just stop worrying about it.

I dial Dan's number.

"Ava-Flava! You made it home?"

"Hey. Yes, I'm here. I had a great time tonight."

"Me, too. We're going to have to get in some more great sessions before you leave."

"Yeah, we will. Well, I'd better get ready for bed. I have an early meeting tomorrow."

"Okay, goodnight."

"Goodnight."

I've taken my bath and am in the bed. Do not text him, don't do it.

I have no willpower. I'm texting this long account of our five minutes in the garage tonight.

Me: *Hey so I am lying here in bed and thinking about our last conversation and the she/he thing you said and I was wondering if I should be concerned because if you will recall we agreed to only have sex with each other. I know we have a somewhat unique relationship but we did agree to only have sex with each other so if you are not holding up your end of the deal please just let me know. I won't be upset I just need to know so that I can move on with my life. Thank you.*

Dan: *Really Ava? I'm not even going to respond to this. Goodnight.*

Shit. I just fucked up! I knew it was just a slip up. It was, right? I don't know. I'm always wondering if Dan is faithful in our non-relationship/relationship arrangement. Clearly he gives me a reason not to trust him. Or maybe I'm just wanting a reason not to trust him. And who would he be sleeping with, when he's such an ass? Who else would put up with this? Some other low-self-esteem woman, like me, that's who.

How can I have had so much therapy and still be this damn clueless?

30

Vaginal Dryness

~

Dan hasn't spoken to me in a month and I am about five weeks from leaving. He does this often, the silent treatment, but this time he has a very good reason, maybe. He did text a couple of weeks ago, after I sent the tenth apology, and said everything was all good and we were fine, but clearly he's not ready to see me.

I shouldn't even care at this point; it's been five years and this weird-ass relationship needs to end. Plus, I've begun to experience vaginal dryness and it's irritating as hell. I'm guessing it's from perimenopause and/or stress, as this move is starting to get the best of me. I interviewed people for positions in my dog walking company, even selected people, and then decided I wasn't comfortable leaving a manager in charge while I was on the other side of the country. Maybe if it was up and running for a few years, but not when just starting the business. My dream of the ultimate dog walking company will have to be put on ice for a while. In either case, the stress of it all, plus packing and attempting to toss half my possessions in the process, has me wanting a vacation. So much for my two weeks off for my recovery from surgery the other month. Feels like it never occurred.

I'm taking a break from sorting items in the hall closet. It's amazing how much crap I have accumulated over my time in this house.

"Come on, girls, let's get some fresh air!"

Cleo and Sophie follow me to the backdoor and we head outside. I have a book with me, a classic, *The Power of Positive Thinking* by Norman Vincent Peale. It's really inspiring, and surprising that it was written over sixty years ago. Maybe some inspirational reading will refresh me. Of course, I have my phone with me, so before I open the book, I take a look at my emails. As I move to my wicker loveseat and sit down I see an email from my doctor's office. It notes I have a new message in their online health record system. I know exactly what it is, the STD results. I get tested every year. I've always come up negative, expect the one time Dan and I reunited after we took a break, oh, and the many times I had chlamydia when I was dating the crackhead in Oklahoma.

I log in to my account and see the results. I am negative for everything. I am not shocked since if I weren't, my doctor would have called me by now, but there's something comforting about seeing it in black and white. Plus, it confirms that this is indeed vaginal dryness and not some Dan-given STD.

I pick up my book to begin reading, but stop and pick my phone back up. I send a quick text to Dan to let him know I'm STD-free with some lame excuse for informing him of this.

Me: *Hey, just got my annual STD results and I am negative on everything. Just thought you'd like to know.*

To my surprise Dan responds immediately: *Cool, thanks for letting me know. So, is this your way of saying you want me to come over and fuck you?*

I can't even get pissed at his response, as I am not remotely surprised. It's such a shame he hides his feelings behind this sex shit, and he has to know he's transparent. I will never understand him.

Me: *I thought you lost interest in fucking me.*

Dan: *Why would you think that?*

Me: *Because I haven't heard from you in awhile.*

Dan: *Oh.*

I have lost any desire to curl up under the beautiful warm sun and read my book. I am almost sick with this text exchange. Why do I do this to myself?

Me: *Maybe we can meet up in a few days. My period is on now.*

Dan: *I can fuck you in your ass.*

Me: *No, thank you. It's been so long I want to enjoy you in every part of me.*

Dan: *Yeah, you do.*

Good, that put him off for a while.

Now, let's read. I feel better, not as nauseated. I see Cleo is sunbathing just outside the perimeter of the umbrella and Sophie has brought me her ball to play fetch. This is the life. Maybe I'm better off with just the three of us. No men allowed.

31

Cleansing

~

I'm with Sheryl sitting in a medical office in Friendship Heights on a Tuesday. She's asked me to join her to at IHC, the Integrative Healing Center, to discuss a body cleanse. I'm not interested in this at all, but I am in need of a break from Shawshank, so I took the afternoon off to join her.

I'm trying my best to pay attention to the conversation between Sheryl and Amy, the health practitioner, but my interest in this subject does not exist. I love food and I can't imagine not eating for any extended period of time, plus cleansing equals more bowels movements and I don't have time in my day to be running to the restroom to relieve myself.

As the video Amy was playing wraps up, I do my best not to squirm in my seat like a disinterested child.

"Do you have any questions?"

Sheryl starts down her list and I smile. I have no questions and, ironically, am starving at this point. As Sheryl and Amy talk, I begin thinking about Dan. I am now a month away from leaving and I don't know if I will see him again. I am also thinking I need to let Dr. Smith know I'm leaving town. The fact that we have weekly sessions and I've yet to bring this up to her is one more reason why I am certain I will be in therapy at ninety-five. I can't decide if I'm not telling her because I don't want to face the questions she'll ask about how I feel and have I thought about seeing someone while I'm out there. The answer is, I don't know. I don't know how I feel, except this is a great opportunity, and the government is paying for everything. I'd be crazy to not go, and I have nothing real with Dan, so leaving him behind is not a factor in this decision at all. Yes, it's a new city, but it's really just a work assignment and I'll be back in a year. It literally is called an extended TDY (temporary duty). This fellowship is my launching point, my ticket to GS-15 and then SES. I don't have any choice but to go. Who would be crazy enough to turn down an all-expense-paid trip to Southern California?

Sheryl and Amy are coming to the end of Sheryl's list of questions, and I slowly bring myself back into the conversation.

"So, Amy, what other services do you provide here?"

"I'm a life coach and I do energy work. I am also a licensed hypnotherapist."

I'm curious. "What exactly is energy work?"

"It's the passing of healing energy from the Source to my clients. It has been known to heal emotional issues, stress, and overall bring the body back into balance."

I'm intrigued. "Really?"

"Yes, it's a wonderful way to recharge."

Amy continues to explain, and I'm drawn to this. She notes chakra balancing, which I only understand from an episode of Dr. Oz, but the show was quite interesting. I wonder if this is what I need. Therapy sure doesn't seem to be the answer. What if what I need is already inside me and I just need a little tune-up or something?

I can tell Sheryl is now in role reversal and is as disinterested in this discussion as I was about the cleansing, so I politely thank Amy for the information and we rise to leave.

"Oh, if you are interested, there is a natural health expo this weekend sponsored by Pathways."

Amy begins to share more about the expo, but as she does I can tell Sheryl and I both are not disinterested. I was all about the energy work, but now she's talking about healing crystals, mediums and other things that don't align with my Baptist upbringing or my adult conversion to United Methodist.

We thank Amy once again and head out.

"I'm starving!"

"Me too! How about going to Whole Foods?"

"Sounds great. "We walk in silence for a few minutes and then Sheryl speaks.

"I'm all about the cleanse."

"I'm not, but I wish you luck!"

"Really, we can be cleansing buddies!"

"I'll pass, thanks."

As we enter Whole Foods, Sheryl explains how she came to find the IHC and her new discovery of holistic health care. I know nothing about this, other than some acupuncture I've had a few times, but I'm always open to learning something new.

We've made our way around the buffet tables and both have fried chicken on our plates—rather comical after listening to Amy discussing cleansing for the last hour. We make our way to an empty table and say grace prior to eating. I love that about Sheryl. She's going to say grace anywhere. I do too, even at the airport sitting at a gate about to dig into a pre-made turkey sandwich.

"Now, Ms. Ava, how's the packing going?"

"It's going great. I've gotten rid of so much stuff and only plan to put a few things in storage for the year."

"Great!"

"Yeah, I want to return next year and start anew."

"So, how is Dan?"

"We haven't spoken in over a month, but it's my fault."

"Really?"

"Yeah, long story. He says everything is fine, yet he doesn't want to be around me. Anyway, I don't want to bring this beautiful day down talking about five-year-old drama."

"Okay, as long as you're good."

"I'm good. I'll be better once I'm settled in Santa Monica and at Big Brains."

"Yeah, well, I'll be sure to come out and visit. Do you have a place yet?"

"Yes, one block from the beach and two blocks from Big Brains!"

"Oh, yes! I'll be visiting you a few times!"

"I'm all for that! You and I can take the TMZ tour!"

"Really, Ava?"

"Yeah, really, it's something I really want to do. That, and go to a taping of the talk show, *The Real*."

"I'm with you on *The Real* and only because I love you, TMZ too."

"Awesome!"

32

Unsuspending Facebook

~

So many people are asking me to let them know how the trip goes, to let them know when I've made it safely from state to state, that I've decided to un-suspend my Facebook account and post every day of my trip out to California. This will be much easier than calling and texting a bunch of people every night.

I think I'll get started a little sooner and show off my new weave. This is such a great selfie, I'm going to change my profile picture, which has been the dogs for years, and show off Monique's awesome skills. I've been good at lying to her about the device. She really believes it's working and since she has no real way to test it—she noted this at my last appointment—she can't find me out. I would have thought, though, she'd be more curious about how it's working, and found some way to test it, but I guess she figures since her own device is doing great, so is mine.

Facebook, May 30 2015
Going to miss my beautiful backyard but my journey begins soon so I'll enjoy it as much as I can until I leave but...I do get to trade it in for an apartment that's a block from the beach!!!

Facebook, June 7 2015
My lil helper! I have partnered with one of my clients who makes dog blankets which I will sell as part of my online store. She gave Cleo and

Sophie their own and Sophie put it to the test! I feel good knowing we are
selling a quality product!

I love this You Tube video. Sophie fluffing up this crocheted blanket is
just adorable! And, it is proof that these things are indeed durable. I can
see them selling quickly and becoming a world-wide hot item.

I do this a lot. Daydream. There's nothing wrong with it, but in an
instant, fear floods me, and so it stays just that most times—a dream.
But, I am determined to make something out of this business. I may be
putting the dog walking/pet sitting piece on hold, but I can have my
online store and it should be easy enough to run from California. We'll
see.

> *Facebook, June 12 2015*
> *You can't base your life on other people's expectations*
> *– Stevie Wonder*

What a fantastic quote! Although that's all I've done so far, based my
life on other people's expectations…but, maybe Stevie Wonder will also
inspire one of my fifty Facebook friends. I don't have a lot of them. I
mainly only have family, friends and a select group of co-workers who
popped up after I unsuspended my account. But, it's all good, as I am
only going to keep it unsuspended until I get out to California. I'm not
a Facebook person and only got an account a few years ago for an Air
War College study group.

Facebook, June 16 2015
Post of Earnestine Shepherd, a seventy-nine year old body builder.

Seeing Earnestine has inspired me. I think I'm going to—no, I am going to get a personal trainer when I get out there. I will be able to afford it since I'll be living on per diem. This will be good for me, getting back in shape, like when I worked out with my friend, Mike. I know I can get that look back pretty quickly. I had the pleasure of seeing this fabulous woman a few years ago at one of Mike's competitions and she has been my motivation ever since! Hopefully she will inspire those who are wanting to get in or stay in shape!

Facebook, June 19 2015 (Juneteenth)
At Uplift Spa – facelift session

I found this place on Groupon. I'm a bit of a Groupon addict. I have this belief that if I spruce up my looks, Dan will finally admit his love for me and want a more traditional relationship. I spend a lot of money in this place every week and while there is a noticeable difference in the bag that has been under my right eye since birth, I think I could be spending my money more wisely. I doubt Dan has even noticed the difference.

Facebook, June 29 2015
Well it's about time to hit the road! Two more days, then off to something new and exciting! Thank you God for this amazing blessing!!!

There is now an echo in this house. The storage company has hauled everything away that I didn't toss in the trash or have the junk company come for last week. It's bittersweet. I love this house and I will miss this neighborhood, but I'm going to freakin' Santa Monica! I am sad to be leaving Dan, too. He's stopping by tomorrow before he heads out of town with the senator. I am toying with whether to ask him about our status. Do we see other people while I'm gone? This isn't a real relationship, so I guess I already know the answer, but it saddens me. Damn me for holding on to this weird shit for five years. I have no one to blame but myself. I've had many opportunities to walk away, and I have, and then I'm back. Why is it that every man I date doesn't measure up to Dan? They suck at good conversation, and they have no clue about current events. Even the sex is bad. I always end up back with Dan. He once said to me this would always be the case, that we are destined to be together, but not in some romantic way, in some "we are both really fucked up" kind of way. I am still holding out the hope that he is wrong about this, but if I'm honest, I kind of hope it's true because I don't want to lose him out of my life. Yes, we are both fucked up, but damn we get along wonderfully. We can talk on the phone for hours and when we are together we have a great time, conversation, joking, music. We even sleep well together. He's a great spooner, though Steve Harvey warned in his book, *Act Like A Lady, Think Like a Man*, that a man will go through all of the motions to sleep with you, even cuddle with you, but that doesn't mean he's ever going to take you home to meet his momma. I know this is Dan, but I think I'd rather live in our make-believe world where we act like and look like a couple, but are not. If only I can push past the part of feeling incredibly lonely, it could work.

33

Goodbye

~

It's pouring rain today and I'm at the nail salon. Dan said he'd stop by in a few hours before he heads to the airport for his trip with the senator, and I have it in my head that I must have a fresh mani/pedi for this visit. Though, as I think about it, I've always been on point with this, as I never wanted to give him any reason for finding me unattractive.

I'm heading to the back for my brow wax and I'm so sad. I can't help but think of my last session with Dr. Smith. She asked what were my intentions for therapy for the next year and I boldly told her I had none.

"Are you sure you don't want me to recommend a few of my colleagues?"

"No, but thank you. I think I want to just take a break."

"A break?"

"Yes, I think there will be enough distance between Dan and me that it will be fine."

"Shit, Ava, you are aware that you are not just here because of you and Dan. Dan is…"

"Dan is a symptom, I know, but, well, I'm only going to be out there for a year and I want to enjoy every minute of it and I don't want the burden of having to go to therapy."

"I see. It's too time-consuming?"

"Okay, no, but out there I can just be me and maybe a new routine and new job will do wonders for me."

"It really is up to you."

"Yes, it is."

I know damn well I need to be in someone's office once a week, but just for this short year, I want to live as though I'm one-hundred percent okay. I have a strong belief that this will be the case, which is good because I'm never confident about much of anything.

"Lip, too?"

"Huh, what?"

"You want lip wax, too?"

"No, I don't think so…should I?"

"Oh, honey, yes, it's good to do it."

"Is there hair there?" I'm shocked. I use the hair remover lotion all the time.

"Yes, of course, there is hair, honey. Let me do lip, too. Plus, when you wax, it make the lip look lighter."

"Really? Okay."

Damn, have I been walking around with lip hair all these years? I thought the lotion remover was working. It probably was, or I would have noticed by now. I am so gullible, but whatever. I am rushing to get done. I want to be home before Dan arrives.

"See, honey. You look much better."

"Yes, thank you."

I pay for my services and hop in my car. I get home with about ten minutes to spare before the doorbell rings.

"Ava-Flava!"

"Hey."

Dan is looking very handsome in his light grey suit. He is standing at the door with a big grin on his face and a golf umbrella over his head. I'm casually dressed in a black and green sundress and black flip-flops that show off my OPI Cajun Shrimp nails. My face is free of makeup with the exception of a light touch of foundation and lip gloss, and my weave is a throwback to the late seventies or early eighties (Monique added a flip to my look this time).

"Come in."

"Wow, you cleared this place."

"Yep, nothing left but these boxes for the FedEx guy to pick up in the morning. I'm shipping these to Santa Monica."

"Oh."

Dan is still standing in the entryway. The look on his face is shock and confusion.

"I can't stay, but just wanted to say goodbye. My flight leaves in two hours."

"Oh, okay."

I want to ask about our relationship status, but I'm scared to hear the answer. I have to drive across the country starting tomorrow morning, and I don't need to be an emotional mess because of this question. But, I can't just leave things open-ended. Or, maybe I should; then, if we don't discuss it, we are still together even though we are not really together.

Why do I sound like I'm in high school and not a grown-ass forty-two-year-old woman?

"Well, I'm going to miss you."

"Yeah, me too. But I'll be back next month for the orientation, and you can come visit."

"Yeah, of course."

I have a hard time believing he will, though I selected an apartment one block from the beach, two blocks from the Santa Monica Pier and adjacent to the 3rd Street Promenade, to ensure he'd be well entertained should he visit, and well, honestly, hoping to entice him to come visit.

Dan interrupts my thoughts with a hug. It feels so good I don't want him to let me go. I squeeze him tightly and hold my breath. We stay like this for a few minutes and then he lets go. He looks down and at me and gives me a soft kiss on my lips.

"Have a safe drive. I know you are stopping every evening, and I also know you like to sleep in, but you need to get up early every morning to be sure you get to the next stop before the sun sets."

"Okay, I will."

Dan is protective and thoughtful and, well, a lot like a dad now that I am thinking of it. He has helped me with everything from my Thrift Savings Plan allocation to selecting new tires for the 4 Runner I owned. He even insisted I have the property manager send me pictures of the apartment I will be living in to confirm it was as good as the photos on their website. He has to love me if he does all this, right? Plus, the oatmeal and tongs from the other month.

He gives me one more quick hug and kiss, and then grabs his umbrella. As he opens the door I feel a lump in my throat and my heart sinks. I follow him out and stand under the awning.

"I will check in with you each night."

"Yeah, you'd better. Don't have me tracking you down across the country."

"Have a safe trip."

"You, too."

He hurries down the stairs and hops into his car. I can't bring myself to move. Things are never going to be the same between us, and I know this. Not that they were ever great, but this break in our friends-with-benefits arrangement is going to change us forever.

Or not. Stop being so damn negative, Ava. You get what you put out there. Stop putting out bad vibes.

I didn't ask my question. I couldn't. I wanted to have a good memory of us saying goodbye, but now, not even ten minutes later, it's eating me alive and I need to know where things stand.

Don't call him, Ava. Don't do it. Just drive out there and play it cool. I bet if you do he will come out to visit and it will be okay. If you call him and bring this up you are going to spook him and that whole commitment thing will be in his head. He doesn't want a relationship, but you've got exclusive, sex-only, friends-with-benefits going, so chill, and who knows you may get out there and meet Shemar Moore and he falls madly in love with you and you won't give a damn about Dan.

My phone is ringing. It's Dan. That's odd, since he just left.

"Hey, what's up?

"Hey, just wanted to remind you to walk the dogs in very open public places when you stop to take breaks."

Oh yes! See, he really does care. Never mind I drive to South Carolina and Alabama all the time with the dogs and he's never once concerned himself with my safety at rest stops. This is a sign to ask my question.

"Okay, thanks. I will be sure to do that. Um, have you thought about what you want to do while I'm gone?"

"Do what?"

"Our agreement?"

"Oh, you know, Ava, I don't want to be with anyone else but you."

Yes!

"But, since you brought it up, we should just reset after you get back. A year is a long time to go without sex, right?"

"Right? I thought you'd come visit though?"

"Yeah, but you know I'm transitioning out of this Hill job back to real estate, so my time to travel will be limited."

"Oh, of course."

"It's just a year, and I'll be here for you when you get back."

"Sure, well, thanks for letting me know."

"Yeah, sure."

"Bye."

"Bye."

I am feeling so much more with this damn device being stuck in right-brain mode. I really should've asked Monique to fix it. I can't believe I've been lying to her all this time about how great it's working. Anyway, I'm not crying, so that's good. I just feel numb, dumb and lonely. Probably not a good thing, though. Sure this fellowship looks great to others. To most people it would look like I'm the shit, with my new fancy car, apartment a block from the beach, and a year away from Shawshank—but something's wrong.

I'm not sure what I want, but I know what I have doesn't look anything like what everyone has said I should have by this time in my life. I'm starting another chapter in my life again, alone.

I'm so tired of this shit, so tired of this illusion. I must discover the real Ava.

* * *

DON'T MISS THE NEXT BOOK IN THE
SERIES OF AVA MCCLURE'S JOURNEY

ENJOY THIS SPECIAL PREVIEW!
From the Soon-to-be-Published

BOOK TWO

ENLIGHTENED

The Lady and Her Pentagon

1

What Lies Ahead

~

Although I had lived in that house for five years, there's no emotional downside to leaving, as the Landlord was quite an ass right before I moved out, wanting to fix things all of a sudden that I had complained about for years. Now, he needed to get them done the week before I headed out of town. He had contractors knocking on my door at the crack of dawn and had the nerve to tell me I couldn't leave the house until the handyman repaired the backdoor and the paint dried. Of course, I kicked the dude out after his first coat of paint. It was the day of my going away party and I had to drive all the way to Waldorf. Oh, well.

He's such an ass, *and* a Republican. He has a bumper sticker that says "Fire Obama"—I can't believe I gave this man rent for five years. I did reply to his last email, though, and made a note of my distaste for his behavior. His wife wrote back apologizing, and told me they enjoyed me as a tenant, not to worry about any more repairs, and to have a safe trip. I don't speak up for myself often enough, so that email sure felt good.

In any case, we're leaving now. The dogs are in the car and I've quadruple-checked everything and I'm dropping the keys into the mail slot back through the door.

This shit is over.

We're heading down to South Carolina for a couple of days to see my parents and then on to California. I am ready for this new chapter of my life, but yet, a little sad. After Dan stopped by yesterday to say his goodbye, I don't know what I'm feeling other than completely unsure of what the year will bring for us. I'll be back next month for the fellowship orientation. I just hope he'll want to see me since we are taking a friends-with-benefits hiatus for the next year.

Perhaps I should just let it go now and start anew. Perhaps be completely free, with my heart wide open, so that when I meet Shemar there will be no hang-ups (a fantasy, yes, but I am heading to the LA area for a year, so why not dream). I love the thought of meeting Shemar Moore while I'm out there, and of us falling madly in love with each other. It could happen, as celebrities do sometimes date regular people. And, I could retire my vibrator for good!

More realistically, I can't believe I'm leaving town without telling Monique that this LR-7 device is not working, but I've been pretty much zenning in right-brain mode, so to hell with it, I'm going to California this way. And, it's a fellowship, not a real job. Now I'm playing devil's advocate. I have this device in my head and the controller in my arm. Maybe I should've gotten a tune-up or something before leaving the area. Instead, I just got my hair done and lied about it operating correctly. I don't know…maybe make time to see Monique while I'm back for the orientation next month…or maybe I won't.

Facebook, July 4 2015

As we celebrate Independence Day, I can't help but be reminded of all the wonderful things that I was able to experience in and around our nation's capital. These are just a few of those great things that were still saved on my phone 😊

Facebook, July 5 2015

Made it to Memphis! Celebrated the 4th with my family in SC then hit the road this morning...ready for food and bed!

Facebook, July 5 2015

Question??? anyone know what happens to all the new bottles of ketchup after they are barely used? Seems like a waste...but I get that it's room service so packets would be tacky 😄

Facebook, July 6 2015

Late checkout = late arrival to Oklahoma City. We are pooped! But as I was driving through...oh my goodness even in the dark I can see some pretty cool changes over the last eight years! Shout out to my Tinker crew!

Facebook, July 7 2015

Just rolled into Albuquerque! The odometer reads 2200 miles for this trip from VA to SC to TN to OK to NM! This is an awesome road trip! Almost there!!!

Facebook, July 8 2015

Made it to Phoenix!!! It is sooo hot! Too many years on the East Coast has desensitized me to 100+ degree weather! Gave up sightseeing and came back to my very cool hotel room.

Facebook, July 9 2015

We are done!!! We are in Beautiful Santa Monica! Thanks to all of you for your thoughts and prayers! Looking forward to a great year at Big Brains Inc.!

We've arrived! It's early afternoon and an insatiably beautiful sunny day. There was a mix-up with the move-in date for the apartment, and since I have to report to Big Brains on Monday, I booked us a room at the JW Marriott Santa Monica Le Merigot. To date, this will be the fanciest hotel I've stayed in.

I pull into the driveway of the hotel where a bellhop greets us. I'm exhausted and tired, but yet happy and relieved, and I am a ball of emotions, but I must keep moving forward. All I want to do is get the car unpacked, take the girls for a quick walk, and get a good meal and a good sleep. I still have to arrange for the utilities in the apartment to be turned on, and I need to report to work on Monday, but I have a good two-and-a-half days to become familiar again with Santa Monica. It's been a few years since I was last here on TDY, and for those trips, I didn't venture past the Promenade.

"Good afternoon! Welcome to Le Merigot."

I smile and I can feel my eyes sparkling with delight through my sunglasses. I can tell I'm already getting the big head with this type of attention.

"Thank you."

"Let me help you. Will you need everything from the vehicle?"

"Unfortunately, yes, as we will be staying for a week."

"No problem, ma'am."

I pop the trunk and he begins to unload the car. As he does, I go to the back seat to unbuckle Cleo and Sophie. As usual, they have been the best companions. These two are truly my road dogs.

I enter the hotel with Cleo, Sophie and the bellhop who is pushing our belongings behind us. My weave is on point and I'm dressed in a royal blue maxi dress and sandals. You can't tell me I'm not Elle Woods from *Legally Blonde*, only I'm reversing it, and arriving on the west coast rather than the east.

As I reach the counter, the bellhop hands me two bottles of water.

"For the dogs, ma'am. You'll find sparkling water in the room for you."

"Why, thank you." My smile could shatter the windows in this place. First day in California in this fancy hotel, and the bellhop gives me free water for the dogs. I feel like a rich person. I feel like part of the elite.

Ben, the bellhop, has gotten us settled into our room. I am impressed that he took all of this junk out of the car and got it on one of those little carts. As I'm tipping him (I hope ten dollars is a good tip) he's handing me more bottles of water for the girls. I'm feeling special. I'm feeling a little bit above myself. I'm in this awesome hotel by the beach and I have a bellhop hooking me up with extra sundries.

"Thanks again for your help, Ben."

"You are welcome, Ms. McClure. Enjoy your stay."

Life is pretty good right now. I can't wait to get the girls out for a walk, find something good to eat for lunch, and take a short nap. I can't rest long, though, as I have to get everything going to get the utilities on in the apartment. I want everything done as soon as possible because I know this year is going to fly, and I want to be settled quickly so that I can really enjoy this year. Thank you, God, for this opportunity!

As we enter the elevator to head out for a walk, a wave of sadness overcasts my Lifestyles of the Rich and Famous moment. Dan. I thought he loved me, but he's blown me off since I started heading west. I've called or texted every day of our journey and nothing until last night in Phoenix. I'm pretty sure the only reason I received a response was because I played the woe is me card. I sent him an email telling him I was nervous about coming out here:

I've been trying to contact you all week and nothing. I'm heading out to the other side of the country to do this new thing. I don't know anyone out here and this is a big deal to me. I needed your support. I thought you wanted to know how I was doing each day? Why are you ignoring me? I'm all alone and I just need a friend.

He emailed me back a pep talk:

Sorry, Ava, been busy. Showing homes and making a name for myself in the real estate game. You're going to do fine. You're Ava-Flava! Starting something new is not hard—you just have to start. Take care.

The day before I left he said he didn't want to be with anyone else but me, and here we are a week later, and he's ghosted out on me. In either case, I'm determined to not let this ruin my time out here. I'm excited that I will meet the other fellows in a couple days, and will move into my apartment a few days after that.

I feel somewhat unsure and insecure, but I feel pretty damn good, too. This is my year and I'm going to make the best of it. I'm going to enjoy everything there is to do here in California! To hell with Dan's ass. We've parted ways before and I didn't die. This time will be no different.

The girls and I head down Main Street and begin our walk. I am blessed to be here. I'm in California for a year—how could it be anything but a blessing?

2

California State of Mind

~

There are many things I could be doing tonight, playing with the girls, writing, reading or just being a couch potato, but none of these things won out. Today I took time from my not-so-busy evening and wandered up Santa Monica Boulevard to a quaint little bookstore. I've passed this store several times, but never went inside. From a quick glance each time I could see it was a spiritual bookstore, and by "spiritual," I mean the most noticeable thing inside was a very large statue of Buddha. No, not spiritual like my folks back in Alabama would think; in no way is it a "Christian" bookstore.

I've been searching for my space, my place where I could truly connect with God. Just two months ago, while back in DC for a conference, I found myself lying on a medical table in Friendship Heights receiving energy reading and healing, which I now understand as Reiki and undergoing Affect Bridge Hypnotherapy. And while I don't have the words for it, I know my soul is aching for newness. It requires more than Sunday morning church services and more than counseling with a pastor would ever yield, and while the Reiki and hypnotherapy has worked, I knew I'd have to find something to help maintain my new energy flow.

So, here I am on a random night in November by happenstance of seeing a local meet-up invite in my email. As I enter the Bolt of Lightning Spiritual Bookstore it is early, so I have a chance to look around. The store is dimly lit, small, and every space inside is covered with books, crystals and essential oils; every element in this space has its own residence, or rather temporary residence, as it awaits its new owner to claim it and give it a new home. The book titles alone seem to be filling my soul with a much-needed dose of love. From chakra balancing to yoga practices to the healing power of crystals, they are all here and they welcome me into this space.

I find the tiny staircase hidden at the back of the store. As I slowly climb each step, I look around and take it all in; downstairs now looks like a sea of books and artifacts with the beautiful statue of Buddha adding droplets of light to the room, and upstairs is still a mystery. As I make my way upstairs to the meeting area I feel a sense of peace. No thoughts are entering my mind, only vibes that would normally help me realize I was out of my element. Nothing is urging me to head back downstairs and go home.

I find my place on the floor and wait for others to arrive. As I sit waiting in this tiny loft area, I read more book titles, from Jesus to Karma. All of what anyone could ever think to find an interesting spiritual subject is here in this space.

She appears. Grace in form of a beautiful woman. She walks with ease, she smiles with ease. She seems to be floating around us though she has seated herself in front of the group on the floor. I can feel my soul devouring her essence. I want her peace and tranquility. I am hungry for her words, yet I feel a sense of patience as we wait for a few others to find their way to the floor. She then speaks.

She tells of her discovery of meditation and the joy that now encompasses her life. She offers truth in the time and effort required to establish a good practice. She is done. She is brief with her words and yet it is so clear why I am here. I tried meditation in the past—bought a book, downloaded an App—but it didn't work.

After her talk I approach her. I need this now. I fill out the form and we discussed good dates for my class to begin. Walking home I am relieved. This is the missing link; I know it is. That was it. It was short and to the point and I know this is what I need next in my journey. Everything is coming so easily to me since my Reiki session. I don't stress; I just *am* and it just comes.

It's seven o'clock and I'm a good fifteen minutes away from her home. I don't want to panic as this is my first session and that doesn't seem like the best way to start a four-day mediation course. She said not to worry and to take my time, but all I know is I hate being late. I left my place over an hour ago thinking I had more than enough time. I hate LA traffic, yet this city is beginning to grow on me and I am starting to think I should stay here after my fellowship ends this summer.

The GPS has directed me to take a right. I am now on her street; just need to find a place to park. Okay. I'm only ten minutes later than our start time. Somehow this makes me feel better, but I am certain it stems from insecurity.

As I approach the door I see the sign asking guests to remove their shoes. As I begin to remove mine, she appears at the door. She is doing it again, that ease of her smile, that warmth that I've never felt around another human being before. Oh, please God, let me get this good vibe; let it be a part of my existence after finishing this course.

I have brought a few items for our first session, as requested in her email to me—flowers, a white napkin, and a piece of fruit. I hand them to her and she begins to explain the offering. After the offering she begins to explain Vedic Mediation and its origins with Maharishi Mahesh Yogi, and gives me my mantra.

We end the first session with a meditation session. I close my eyes and allow my mantra to come to me. After some time she tells me to let go of the mantra and to slowly open my eyes.

"How do you feel?"

"Good, peaceful. I did feel the numbness you noted."

"Good. Did you see anything?"

"No, just an almost paralyzing sense of stillness."

"That's good and especially for your first time. You can meditate on your own in the morning and we'll do your evening mediation tomorrow during your next session."

"Okay, great."

"You have such a peaceful energy."

"Really, I do?"

"Do you not think so?"

"I guess I thought I was always feeling rushed, but since moving here in July, yes, I guess I have less stress in my life. It makes me want to stay here and not return to the DC area."

"If that's what you want to do, you should do it."

"Yes, I should."

I smile as she walks me to the door. I give her a hug and walk outside. As she closes the door, I slip on my shoes and I can feel the big grin making its way across my face. I don't know if it's the mediation or her exceptionally calm nature that has me so at ease. I just meditated and it felt amazing! Something was happening to me, to my body and my soul. I had felt the numbness on my lips as she said I might. I felt an overwhelming sense of peace and stillness.

It didn't take four sessions for me to start feeling the positive effects of mediation. By the end of night two, I was driving home singing along with the radio and radiating all kinds of positive energy.

Nala was impressed with how quickly I took to the practice. She said most of her students normally didn't see such immediate effects. I am now seeing beautiful colors when I meditate and I've transcended a few times. The transcending is amazing, really indescribable. Twice a day for twenty minutes has drastically changed me.

I want to encourage everyone to learn mediation.

I can't imagine anyone's soul not needing this.

* * *

Will Southern California be a new beginning for Ava?
What will a year away from the Pentagon, Dan,
and the life she's known for so many years yield?
Will she ever tell Monique about the broken LR-7 device?

How far can Ava's new life take her toward where she wants to be?

This is only the beginning...